Julian Madigan and his father, co-author, Gerry Madigan both live in Dublin. Julian having survived his narrow escape with drugs is back into competitive sport. Gerry set up Paragon Communications in 1989 which runs courses on leadership development.

The Agony of

ECSTASY

The Agony of

ECSTASY

JULIAN MADIGAN

POOLBEG

Published 1996
by Poolbeg Press Ltd
123 Baldoyle Industrial Estate
Dublin 13, Ireland

© Julian Madigan

The moral right of the author has been asserted.

A catalogue record for this book is available from the British Library.

ISBN 1 85371 682 0

Cover photography by Mark Nixon and Mike O'Toole
Cover design by Poolbeg Group Services Ltd
Set by Poolbeg Group Services Ltd in Garamond
Printed by The Guernsey Press Ltd,
Vale, Guernsey, Channel Islands.

ACKNOWLEDGEMENTS

This book wouldn't have been written except for the help, support and encouragement I received from my family, my coach Eddie McDonagh, my counsellor Mary Cantwell Lynch, and the constant nagging from my father.

A special thanks to my editor, Kate Cruise O'Brien for having faith in me, for her patience and diligence with the red pen, and for listening.

I wish to acknowledge the support I received from Marina, Liam Nicholson, Christy McEnerney, Liam Gallagher, Joe Shannon, and all at YSA. A special thanks to Elder Conk and Elder Wilson for their time and dedication in helping me get on the right track.

To all at Poolbeg for believing in me, helping me get the work done and making this book a reality.

To my mother and Paul for their patience. And of course my dad, without whom I would not be where I am today, and this book would not have been written. I wish to thank all those who helped me this past year in so many ways during my recovery – you know who you are.

I wish to express my sincere sympathy to the parents and friends of all those victims who have died from drug abuse. I hope that this book will help in some small way to prevent other young people from suffering a similar fate. I'm lucky to have broken free from the drug culture, and to still have the ability to engage in sport – I'm grateful to be alive.

For my Grandmother

CONTENTS

LETTER FROM MARY CANTWELL LYNCH

Julian's Counsellor

Julian Madigan first came to see me in October of 1994. It is difficult to describe him accurately but let me just say that, if I had a daughter, I certainly would not like to see her bringing him home to meet me. If I had a son whom he came to visit I wouldn't be too impressed either. However, all of this was just on initial appearance and first impression.

After our first session I realised that I was dealing with a very hurt, angry young man with whom it was difficult to communicate in any emotional way. He was guarded, but he always told me the truth, which was a breakthrough in itself.

He was "using" drugs, and I don't like to classify any drug as hard or soft. The fact was that he was "using" and he didn't see any good reason why he

1

should stop. He was having a good time enjoying life in his own way . . . living close to the edge.

Julian always attended the counselling sessions in body at least. He was on the road to destruction, but no one could tell him that. He thought he could stop whenever he wanted. In his own mind he was immune to addiction. He had already seen what drugs had done to some of his friends, but that could never happen to him!

Like many young people, Julian believed that anyone over the age of twenty-five was old and hadn't got a clue about real life as it is today. He was in control of his drug use, the drugs were not in control of him. At least that's what he said.

His young life was not happy and, like a great many addicted people, he was "using" to kill past pain and boost his confidence. His grandmother had recently died, which upset him greatly, and he was able to express some emotion about that.

Counselling with this young man had to be non-judgmental, and at the same time directional. I built up a relationship with Julian by offering support, and getting him to recognise his feelings and then to express them.

Then came the time when Julian ran into a crisis situation with a drug dealer. He received a very bad eye injury and, after the initial confrontation with his father, he contacted me in an effort to solve this problem. In consultation with his father the three of us set about addressing and resolving this serious and potentially dangerous problem.

Now the real counselling started. Julian at last realised the seriousness of his situation, and he wanted to change his life. He could see how drugs were damaging his young life. The road to recovery was not going to be easy but, with the support and encouragement of his family, he attended weekly sessions of counselling. He successfully did "inner child" work, went back to sport, and found religion.

Inner child work is painful, and you have to be disciplined in order to complete the journey. Julian took on this task with great enthusiasm. He faced the pain of his past, got in touch with himself, and came out at the other end of his dark tunnel smiling. The REAL Julian had emerged!

Many books have been written on the subject of drugs and drug abuse. This book is *different* because it details the journey of a young person who went from "using" to addiction, then to dealing, and finally to recovery in a relatively short period of time. It is the true story of a life that was on the way to destruction, but with help, support and counselling became a life of success.

I began by saying that if I had a daughter I wouldn't have liked her to bring Julian home as her boyfriend. Now I regret that I don't have one.

With family support, his renewed interest in sport, his new-found religion and counselling, Julian has grown to be a wonderful young man with whom anyone would be proud to be associated.

Mary Cantwell Lynch
Counsellor
ALFA Advisory & Counselling Services

LETTER FROM EDDIE McDONAGH

Julian's Coach

The young man who stood before me had a gaunt wan look about him with a slightly vacant stare. He seemed uncertain of himself as he shook my hand. I immediately liked the firmness of his handshake and knew instantly that I could work with him. I looked at him with what I felt was a kindly fatherly look. He seemed suspicious of my motives, but I hoped he did not sense my bemused inward feelings as I contemplated what I could do to help this young man who was lost in a world that I did not understand.

In all my years working as a JLO (Juvenile Liaison Officer) with the Gardaí I had only dealt with minor offences that did not involve drugs. I was a little fearful that I might fail Julian as he reached out desperately for help in trying to escape from this sub-culture which he had entered, and which in many cases led ultimately to tragedy.

As a coach who has spent the last thirty years in the toughest and most disciplined individual sport of all, I wondered how a mind that was accustomed to a quick pleasurable "fix," and a body, weakened by excesses, would adjust to a tough training regime. My instincts would not allow me to go easy on him because of his background, as I felt that this would do him more harm than good. He must succeed on his own merits or not at all. It would also give me a measure of a principle in which I had long believed – "involvement in sport helps to alleviate boredom, and fills leisure hours with a good, productive and rewarding use of time."

I needn't have worried about Julian's attitude. He was here to get that "monkey off his back," and he threw himself wholeheartedly into the programme which I assigned him. This was to be a gradual build-up over a period of time, and graded to take account of his physical capabilities. Julian seemed to me to be trying to prove himself to himself and to all around him. He had a driving force from within that needed to be focused in the right direction in order to avoid it leading to physical self-destruction.

He seemed to forget that he had been away from training for over two years, and that he could not fit into a training group which had reached the highest possible level of fitness. As a result of his over-zealousness he sustained some muscle injuries in his legs for a short time. This was to be a salutary lesson, and he soon learned that "Rome wasn't built in a day." Within six months he was training at the highest level, and he seemed to thrive on it. So enthusiastic was he about his training that he was capable of winning races at Dublin League level, and he represented the club in the All-Ireland League at senior relay level.

Julian got on very well with all of his team mates, and had a bright and cheerful manner. This helped him and the team to get through many tough track sessions. He reacted well to the successful peer group pressure which is part of the athletic scene. And he enjoyed the camaraderie and "slagging" which is encouraging to all when the going gets tough.

As a younger teenager this same peer pressure had probably caused him to overrate certain friendships and perhaps encourage relationships which, combined with the drugs scene, sees young people drift into destructive practices before they realise it.

That which seems cool, fun and reaches a "high" that is not easily obtainable in everyday life can lead to a dependency which ultimately cannot be controlled, and eventually leads to self-destruction.

Now Julian has found an alternative "high" which has given him a new self-esteem which he will not throw away too easily. This was achieved without any artificial means, and if his cheeks and body are lean now it is because of the physical effort he has been making. In many of my conversations with him during the rest periods from training, Julian expressed the wish to pass on the message which he had learned to those who were still caught up in the drugs net. If it is left to this young man I feel that he will ensure that the hope and quality of life that he has gained *will* be passed on.

In his own way he is a perfectionist. His quest for knowledge, in a sport that has given him hope and self-esteem, is insatiable. His energy level should be translated into a programme to help others find their way out of the quagmire in which they find themselves, and show them that there is light at the end of the tunnel. It is also a measure of Julian's character that he did not allow the injuries which he sustained get to him. After a rest and the proper treatment he returned as enthusiastic as before.

Looking at this healthy young athlete it is hard to believe that he almost pressed the self-destruct button just over a year ago. He was fortunate that he reached out to those who were willing to encourage him back to a worthwhile way of life. Perhaps if parents became aware at an early stage of any drift into the drug culture they could do as Julian and his father have done, and search for help before their sons and daughters reach the dependency stage.

Finally, Julian, it took a lot of guts to face up to your fall from grace, and to accept responsibility for your life. I congratulate you, and wish you continued success as you put the past behind you and face the future with confidence.

Eddie McDonagh
Head Coach
DSD Running Club

CHAPTER ONE

MY INTRODUCTION TO DRUGS

I can still remember the mystery and excitement in the school yard when Senan Dantley pulled a small tinfoil-wrapped substance from his pocket, and I waited to see the real thing . . . drugs!

"Look what I got for changing shifts last night," he said with great excitement.

"What exactly is it?" I asked.

"It's hash, man . . . drugs!"

"Oh yeah . . . hash," I exclaimed. I'd never seen hash before in my life. To tell the truth I wasn't terribly impressed with it, not that I knew what hash was supposed to look like. But this looked like a piece of Bord na Mona briquette. It was about a half an inch square. Brown and dirty looking. As far as I could see it was a very poor substitute for a nice can of Budweiser!

I was fourteen years old. A 500 ml can of beer was more appealing to me than a tiny piece of peat briquette, even if it was the real thing . . . like . . . drugs! I didn't really believe that such a tiny piece of hash could have any real effect on your mood.

My curiosity got the better of me. We talked about the pros and cons of drugs versus beer. One night in Stillorgan we decided to investigate this mysterious drug scene and try to buy some hash for ourselves. I was chosen as the one to go out and get the stuff, partly because I knew where to buy it. I went to a Southside Community Centre to buy our first taste of the real thing . . . drugs man!

This wasn't quite as easy or uncomplicated as I'd thought. I went into the Community Centre and searched out a familiar face in the crowd, a someone that I knew could sell me hash. Ironic that Alcoholics Anonymous were holding a meeting in the Centre that night! I found the guy that I was looking for in the kitchen.

"How are things, John?" I said, trying to be as nonchalant as possible.

"All right, Madzer, what's the story man?" he replied in his Bob Geldof accent.

"Any chance of sorting us out with a ten-spot . . . man?" I said. A ten-spot meant ten pounds worth of hash.

"Aw I don't know, Madzer, there's a bit of a drought on at the moment. It would take me a while to get it for you . . . I'd have to go over to Ashlawn Wall in Ballybrack."

"That's fine with me, John, but roughly how long would it take?" I asked. My friends were waiting anxiously in Stillorgan for me to come back from my first drugs mission.

"I'm just waiting for a guy to come here with some more money for hash. As soon as he comes, I'll go over to Ballybrack, and I should be back within half an hour. Is that OK with you, Madzer?" said John.

"Sure, I'll wait until he comes," I said.

A few of John's mates decided to chip in a few quid to make the trip worthwhile, after all, a thirty pound deal would be better value than a ten pound deal. I found out later that, when a thirty pound deal is divided three ways, each third is larger than a single ten pound deal. A few moments later John's friend arrived and off he went to buy the hash in Ballybrack. I hung around with John's other mates in the Community Centre until he came back, and their conversation was an eye-opener. These guys were seasoned druggies . . . they knew their stuff!

After forty-five minutes I began to get slightly worried. What would the guys back in Stillorgan be thinking? This was my first drugs run . . . was I being ripped off . . . or did the guys in Stillorgan think that they were being ripped off? The rest of the guys in the Community Centre told me that there was absolutely nothing to worry about . . . John would be back, he wasn't a rip-off merchant. None of this helped, and the cups of tea tasted lousy too.

At last John arrived back with the hash, and we all retreated to the privacy of the kitchen at the back of the Community Centre to divide the deal.

"Sorry for the delay, guys, but I had to wait around for the lads to arrive with the stuff," said John. "But it's really great stuff . . . excellent hash, man!" said he with the authority of an expert. He put the hash on the table for us to see. One of the guys got a knife, heated it, and then divided the deal into three equal portions. I didn't know what he meant by "excellent hash, man." I'd never seen such an amount of the stuff before. It didn't look like peat briquette – it was a yellow/brown colour with touches of green mould around the edges.

"Thanks a million, John," I said.

"Why don't you stall for a few minutes, Madzer, and we'll have a quick spliff?" asked John. I was eager to taste some of this "excellent hash," so I agreed.

Two of the guys went off to the gents toilets to make a couple of joints. We went outside the front door of the Community Centre. When the joint came around to me, I took a toke, and this unusual and pleasant taste came into my mouth. I inhaled it like a normal cigarette but it felt like inhaling a cigar. My first taste of the real thing.

I said goodbye to the guys and cycled back to Stillorgan where the other guys were waiting. As I was cycling, the hash began to take affect. I felt really relaxed with a sort of pleasant fuzziness in my head. It was almost as if I was drunk, but yet I could keep my balance on the bike. I felt in control. By the time I arrived at Stillorgan I was heavily stoned.

"Where were you, Madzer, you've been gone nearly two hours? What kept you, did you get the stuff?" came the questions from an extremely impatient group.

"Cool it guys, everything's okay, I've got the stuff," I said, high as a kite.

"I had to wait for him to go over to Ballybrack to buy the stuff," I said. They'd bought some cider, just in case I didn't come back.

We went over to Kilmacud Crokes field behind the Stillorgan Plaza, and tried to roll a couple of joints. This wasn't as easy as it sounds. None of us had actually rolled a joint before. I'd often seen joints being rolled, but there was a big difference between seeing someone else do it and doing it myself. We eventually succeeded in rolling a halfway acceptable joint and smoked it, washed down with mouthfuls of cool cider. It took about twenty minutes for the stuff to hit us, but when it did hit us . . . "peace man, out here on the perimeter we're stoned." It was like being so drunk that your whole body is totally relaxed. Whatever position you're in feels so comfortable that you don't want to move out of it. The whole world could have tumbled down around me, and I couldn't have cared less! You know the way you feel when you've a bad headache and you take strong pain killers? That's how I felt after I smoked hash. I realised why it's called the "wisdom weed." Besides the fact that it was found on King Solomon's grave, the thoughts and ideas that go through your head are extraordinary. You have arguments with yourself without opening your mouth . . . it's all inside your smoke-filled head. But I didn't feel sick or over-full. This wasn't booze. And the feeling lasted for ages.

At about 11.30 we all decided to call it a night

amidst hysterical giggling. I got the 46A bus home to Monaloe. Let me explain where home was for me then. My parents had separated in 1980, and myself and my dad moved to Monaloe Park Road in Blackrock to live with his mother (my grandmother). I didn't know why my parents separated. I didn't realise that this would be my permanent home for the next fourteen years. But my life in Monaloe was very happy, comfortable. My grandmother – I called her Heidi – (not her real name, but a name I'd given her since I was about two years old) showered me with love and affection. For as long as I could remember, I looked forward to visits to "Heidi's house", and now I lived there.

On the way home I began to feel really drowsy but when I arrived home, boy, did I get the munchies! I felt as if I could eat a horse . . . nobody had told me about this. I cooked up a massive feed of chips, burgers, pizza slices, bread and butter and a pot of tea. As I was cooking it I realised that my co-ordination wasn't exactly 100%. I kept putting things in the wrong place. I tried to put hamburgers in the frying pan but they landed on the hotplate behind it. I seemed to be turning on every hotplate but the right one. Making the pot of tea was a very delicate and precarious exercise, but somehow I managed it. In the middle of all this I heard Heidi get up out of bed. She always did when I came home at night.

"What are you doing, Julian?" she asked. She stared at the massive amount of food which I was cooking.

"Nothing, Heidi, I was just feeling very hungry so I decided to cook myself something to eat." I tried to sound calm.

"But it's after midnight, Julian, and that's an enormous amount of food to be eating before going to bed. You won't be able to sleep," she said.

"Ah I'll be fine, Heidi, I have a pain in my stomach from the hunger."

Heidi went back to bed and I gobbled the food while I watched *Night Time* on television. Then I went to bed. What an experience when I hit the bed. I'd never felt so comfortable in my life before. My pillow felt soft, my duvet was snug and cosy, and my bed was unbelievably comfortable. It felt like sinking into a soft cloud as the mattress and duvet hugged every contour of my body. Was this cloud nine? The dreams I had were extraordinary. Vivid. When I woke up the next morning I expected to have a ferocious hangover. There must be some price to pay for such an enjoyable evening and night. But, to my amazement, I awoke feeling fresh and rested, with no after-effects from the hash or the late night food binge. I said to myself "Hey, this hash is the business, man."

THE BACKGROUND

Let me give you a brief idea of my background. On the 9th October 1975 I was born in Holles Street Hospital in Dublin, not that I remember the incident myself, but my parents tell me that I came into the world screaming. I was the first-born child of Gerard and Yvonne Madigan, who were married just one year previously on the 16th November 1974. My father often tells me that he carried me out of the hospital wrapped in a little blue blanket, and my tiny face looked like a big button in the middle of the blanket. For many years as a child I was nicknamed "buttons" to my extreme embarrassment . . . thank goodness it didn't stick.

My parents were involved in the music business. My father was a musician and singer in his own band – The Cotton Mill Boys. He was also involved in record production and artiste management. My father and mother met during a recording session. My dad was asked to produce an album for this new singer called Tracy, who turned out to be Yvonne Jennings. They developed a close working relationship which eventually led to marriage, which in turn produced me . . . the finished product.

When I was born, we lived in Coolamber Park in Templeogue, but I don't remember very much about my first eighteen months in this world, much less in Coolamber Park. We've driven into the Coolamber estate often since then, and my father has shown me the house, the palm tree which my mother planted in the garden, and the long side wall of the garden which my father built – he got severely burned in the process. The house looks very nice and the pictures of my christening, which took place in the house, look very nice too.

Around the middle of 1977, my parents had a trial separation of about six months. I went to live with my grandmother (Heidi), and then with my mother. The house in Coolamber Park was sold – rather a final decision – and I lived in a flat in Fairview with my mum. I was too small to know what was going on in my parents' marriage. But, at the end of the six months, Dad and Mam got back together again and the three of us moved into a new home in Limetree Avenue, Portmarnock. That's where my first real memories begin.

I can still remember the horsey wallpaper in my bedroom, and the big Muppet Show poster on my wall. A rocking horse called Droopey was my constant plaything. My dad often tells about the morning that he and my mum woke up to the sound of banging. It turned out to be me, dressed up in my little red wellington boots, corduroy cap on my head, on top of Droopey, who was on my bed. I had a stick in my hand and I was galloping to my heart's delight. Nothing terribly unusual about this except for the fact that it was only 5.00 a.m.

My most prized possession was my dog Chad. He was a thoroughbred black and white collie which my dad's friend Paul Glynn had given me, and he was my constant companion and protector. Wherever I walked in the garden or around the estate, I was closely followed by this huge collie. I have never known such an affectionate and placid dog. When I took my bottle I would lie back on top of Chad, but he never growled at me. I can remember taking a bone from his mouth when he was eating it, but he didn't object. Unfortunately we had to return him to Paul, who lived in the Dublin mountains, because he kept escaping from our back garden – even though we had a six-foot wall surrounding the garden. Chad would clear the wall in one jump and then run off to play among the sand dunes at the beach. After the third time he disappeared, it was decided that it was unfair to him to keep him in such a confined space. Once, when he was missing, my dad brought me down to the beach to search for him, and I can remember the thick fog as we called out his name . . . "Chad . . . here Chad." Suddenly we heard the sound of his bark and, within seconds, he bounded into view and jumped all over us with excitement.

We lived in Portmarnock for less than three years, but I can still remember vividly the shape of the rooms, the open staircase, the German Shepherd dog which lived in the house next door, the sunny red kitchen and the two young girls with whom I spent many long days in play. They were happy days. I often remember, when Dad and Mam had visitors, we would all sit out in the sunshine in our back garden. There was a building site directly opposite the house because the estate wasn't finished. I thought it was great fun to run up and down the mounds of earth and gravel beside the enclosed site. My mum thought differently when I came home from my escapades absolutely filthy!

There were always musical instruments and band equipment lying about the place. I came to know the difference between a banjo and a guitar or a pedal-steel guitar. The bands used our house for rehearsals. I came down the stairs one morning to see a complete drum kit assembled in the stairwell. Needless to say, I tried my hand at drumming. I could understand how these guys played their fiddles, guitars and banjos, but the pedal-steel guitar looked very strange altogether . . . more like an electric sewing-machine. That didn't stop me testing my musical talent on the array of instruments at my disposal.

My musical recital was interrupted by my mother who dragged me off the drum-stool, and took the guitar out of my hand. She explained that everybody was asleep and it was time for my breakfast. How was I to know that it was early morning and that most people had just gone to bed?

We had a regular flow of overnight guests in our house. I can remember Bernd and Gundi Peters from Germany, with their son Mark, who was the same age as me. We all went to Dublin Zoo for a day trip. I loved going down the helter-skelter on my stomach. Maybe I always liked to live life close to the edge.

There was a great air of excitement about the house in Portmarnock, always plenty of people calling, dinner parties and music parties. I didn't realise the cause of all this at the time.

Apparently my dad's band, The Cotton Mill Boys, had won *Opportunity Knocks* a few weeks in a row. This was a highly rated talent show on British television.

PARENTS' SEPARATION

In 1980 my parents finally separated. I was four years old and, as you can imagine, I didn't pay very much attention. My parents had their reasons for the separation, but I wish I had been older. I might have been able to understand it then.

I remember the day we left Portmarnock. Somehow I knew that this was the last time I would see my house. I was all dressed up in my Lord Fauntleroy coat and hat (that's what my parents called it!). They thought I looked very smart but I didn't want to wear it. My dad had his van parked in the driveway. He put me into the passenger seat and packed the van with the rest of our belongings. The memory of looking out of the van at the house, knowing that this was goodbye, will always be with me.

The journey from Portmarnock to Blackrock (Heidi's house) is quite long by adult standards. For a four year old it was even longer. I fell asleep. I don't actually remember much of the journey. When we arrived at my grandmother's house, I can remember walking in through the front door, gaping into the kitchen and looking at my grandmother, who had her back turned to me. She was working at the sink in the kitchen. As she turned around her face lit up with delight and she came towards me with a warm welcome embrace and a huge kiss, which left a lipstick mark on the side of my face. She took out her little white handkerchief, wet it with her tongue, and wiped the lipstick off my face like all good grandmothers do! Little did I know that this house was going to be my home for the next fourteen years.

For the first six months in Heidi's house I didn't hear from my mother. She was living in England. I was happy in Monaloe and made a lot of new friends on the road and in the estate. I didn't realise that my parents were separated. I just took it for granted that I saw my mother much less often than my friends saw their mothers.

In September of 1980 I started school in the Ursuline Convent in Cabinteely, which was about a mile and a half from Heidi's house. The school was enormous compared to the little prefab in Portmarnock. Heidi walked me to school every morning and collected me in the afternoon.

I thought it was normal to be living with my dad in my grandmother's house. Heidi took the place of my own mother, and I had regular visits from my uncles, aunt and cousins. There was never any shortage of family to bring me out to the zoo, the cinema, or McDonalds.

I realise now that, before I moved into Heidi's, I had no fixed home. I was always moving about from one place to another, uplifting everything and transporting it somewhere else. In 1975 I lived in Coolamber Park. Then for a short period I moved into Heidi's house, and for a few months with my mother. Once again I moved, this time to Portmarnock. That's where my memories really start. But, after only three years, I moved once more, this time to Heidi's house in Blackrock. That was the last move for about fourteen years.

CHAPTER TWO

by Gerry Madigan

I was quite oblivious to all that was going on at this stage in Julian's life. This was around 1990, and I had moved out of Heidi's house to live on my own in Ballyboden. This was partly to make the break less traumatic when I married Marina in 1992. We planned that Julian would live with me for part of the week, and with Heidi for the rest of the week. However, this did not work out. Julian was still attending a local school and that made it difficult for him to commute at weekends.

In hindsight I realise that I was not monitoring his activities as well as I should have been, but at the time I thought he was making good progress. He seemed to be attending school regularly, and sport was still high on his list of priorities. He trained in the running club every Tuesday, Thursday and Friday night, plus a Saturday morning session. So I thought that he was well occupied in his spare time.

The rave scene worried me at first. I talked to Heidi and Julian about it, but Julian told me he was only interested in the music.

"But what about the reports of drugs being sold openly at these raves, Julian?" I asked.

"Dad, do you honestly believe that I'd get involved in drugs at this stage? What would be the point in me going training with the club every week if I was going to take drugs at weekends?"

Heidi wasn't quite convinced, and asked, "But Julian, most of the crowd at these raves are on drugs. Are any of your friends taking drugs?"

"Heidi, you know the gang. We're all into music and sport. We're not stupid enough to get involved with the druggies," he said.

"But you also said that you didn't smoke, Julian, and I caught you smoking about two months ago," I said.

"And I haven't touched them since. You know that, Heidi." He looked at Heidi.

"Yes, we spoke about cigarettes and how they can damage his health. He has to look after his health if he hopes to have a career in sport," she said.

All of this sounded very plausible and I had no reason to mistrust him. I knew that he was heavily involved in the music . . . his stereo was never switched off. Either I was getting very old, or all the music that he played had the same monotonous sound with that pumping rhythm beating out synthetic percussive sounds. It was never like that when I was producing records.

The reason we lived in Heidi's house in the first place was to give Julian some sort of stability after the series of moves in his early childhood. When I married my first wife, Yvonne, in 1974 it was never our intention to separate. However, in 1977 we had a trial separation. This was the beginning of the disruption in Julian's life. We agreed that he would stay with Heidi for the six-month period, and then we would decide at the end of this time what should be done.

In order to make it a genuine separation, we sold the house in Coolamber Park. Yvonne moved back to her mother's house, and Julian and I moved in with Heidi. Unfortunately, I was extremely busy in the music business at this time, and I had to make weekly trips to England. A couple of months into our trial separation I heard that Yvonne had moved into her own apartment. Two weeks later, when I was on tour in England, she took Julian to live with her in her apartment. I was in England when it happened and I immediately telephoned Yvonne to see what was going on.

"What's the problem, Yvonne? I thought you were going to take Julian for the day and then leave him back to Heidi's house?" I asked.

"He's my son, Gerry, and as far as I'm concerned he's staying with me," she replied.

"Couldn't this have waited until I came home on Friday? I mean, really . . . this is the sort of thing we didn't want to happen. Could you not have discussed it before I came away?" I asked.

"I'm fed up discussing everything about my rights to my child. It's nobody else's business except ours. His rightful place is with his own mother," she said.

"OK. We'll talk about it when I get home. We're coming in on the twelve o'clock flight from London on Friday, so I'll see you then," I said.

This obviously created more friction and contention, but it also brought matters to a head. We had to decide what we'd do at the end of this *trial* separation.

We decided to give the marriage another try. We bought a new house in Portmarnock, and we were all one small happy family again. Shortly after moving into Portmarnock, Yvonne decided to go back into the music business herself. Two of us engaged in the business meant travel, stayovers, late nights, etc., so Julian spent a lot of time with babysitters, or in Heidi's house for long weekends, or with Yvonne's mother.

But there were some very happy times in Portmarnock. We used to bring Julian's dog, Chad, for walks along the sand dunes at the beach, and we had great fun chasing him up and down the dunes. There were often guests in the house, and Julian had plenty of children to play with in the estate. As far as Julian was aware, all was well. But all wasn't well.

Our second attempt at making our marriage work ended two and a half years later. This time we made concrete ground rules with regard to the separation – Julian was to stay with me! It's difficult to pinpoint the reason for the marital breakdown, but I guess we were both very immature. We had different ideas about marriage, and we approached our marriage from opposite directions. There should be some kind of convergent thinking in any marriage, but ours was constantly divergent. I was far from the ideal husband. My wife was not the sole focus of my life. I listened to third parties who were too free with their advice. I never took the time to accept Yvonne for the person that she was, instead of the person I wanted her to be, or thought that she should be. And I wasn't the focus of her life either. We were constantly coming up against issues that drove us apart. We came from different backgrounds and our prejudices put unnecessary pressure on an already fragile relationship. I won't go into the gory details of the separation but, when the dust settled, it worked out fairly well. This time we didn't sell the house. We agreed a financial arrangement. I kept the house. Yvonne went to live in England initially. Julian and I went to live with Heidi.

Julian adapted very well to the new domestic arrangements. He always felt comfortable with Heidi. We tried to make his life as normal as possible. He took a keen interest in swimming. The two of us used to get up at six o'clock every morning for his early morning training sessions in Blackrock College swimming-pool. He did tremendously well at swimming galas and began to think of sport as a career.

When I think back to those early years, and especially the period when he began to dabble in drugs, I shiver with fright at my sheer ignorance. Julian had never given me any trouble when he was small. I never had a problem with other parents or teachers. I had no reason to believe that he would have the slightest interest in drugs, and I didn't want to believe that he would actually take them. He couldn't be that foolish, not after all the talks about physical fitness for excellence in sport. I was one of thousands of ignorant parents worldwide – totally ignorant.

I wasn't naïve enough to think that he wasn't taking the odd drink. He often had a glass of wine with dinner, but I didn't think he was a drinker. I was familiar with the smell of alcohol so I could always detect the smell if he was drinking. As far as I knew he'd given up cigarettes.

In September of 1991 Julian lived with me in Ballyboden from Monday to Friday, and stayed with Heidi on the weekends. He had lost interest in swimming some time before, so he no longer had the discipline of early morning swimming. During that autumn school-term, in an effort to resurrect enthusiasm for early morning discipline, we left our house at 6.30 every morning. We would arrive at Westwood Health Club at 6.45 a.m., and have a workout, run, swim and sometimes a game of squash. This would be followed by showers and breakfast at the club. I would drop him into school at 8.45 a.m. He seemed to be fit and healthy. I should have suspected something when he decided to quit the swimming club. But I listened to his logical explanations about the time-consuming element of swimming, his preference for running, and his apparent concern for his studies.

CHAPTER THREE

THE RAVE SCENE

In the summer of 1990 I went to my first rave. I was hanging around the Bowling Alley in Stillorgan one Tuesday night with a few friends when I heard my name being called from across the road.

"Hiya, Madzer, how's it going man?" I looked across the road and recognised Nigel.

"All right, Nigel, what's happening man?" I said.

"Nothing much really . . . except I was at a rave last Saturday night and it was absolutely kickin'." I'd heard a lot about these raves, but this was the first guy that I knew who'd *been* at one.

"What was the music like?" I asked.

"It was really good, man, I've never seen anything like it over here before. They played loads of English hard-core dance that's not even available on vinyl in this country," he said.

"That sounds class, man. Is there another one on soon again?" I asked.

"Yeah, there's one this Saturday . . . would you be interested?"

"Of course I'd be interested, definitely, man," I said.

We arranged to meet in Stillorgan on the next Saturday to go into town to my first rave.

I spent the next four days trying to imagine what this rave would be like. I'd seen some clips on television about them in England, and they looked absolutely amazing. It was only four days until the rave, but the days seemed to drag. On Saturday night I met Nigel in Stillorgan at 8.30 p.m. and we hopped on a 46A bus into town. The excitement was killing me. I kept asking him questions about it all the way into town. I was like a little kid being brought to the circus for the first time, but this was a very different type of circus!

We arrived in town and we headed down Grafton Street to McDonalds to meet a few of Nigel's friends. When we arrived at the rave I wasn't very impressed with the building. It was extremely old and scruffy-looking on the outside, but there was quite a crowd gathered around the entrance. The door was manned by about four dodgey-looking bouncers in their fifties. One had slicked-back greasy grey hair in a pony-tail.

The crowd outside wore the same sort of clothes – coloured jeans, baggy tops and Fila, SPX or Champion runners, and rucksacks on their backs. Most of the guys had typical Manchester haircuts. They all wore whistles around their necks, why I didn't know at that time.

Suddenly the music started pumping. You could almost feel the power of the base line even though we were still outside. The shutters went up. Nigel and I joined the crowd as it surged forward towards the pay-hatch. This was supposed to be an over eighteens rave, I was fifteen, but they didn't ask for any ID at the door. We each paid our four quid and were searched lightly by the bouncers. We headed for the main dance floor and sat at the side of the stage on the built-in seating which circled the dance floor. Within a few minutes the place started to fill up, and we joined the crowd on the floor to strut our stuff.

The smell of hash drifted across the dance floor. We went upstairs to the balcony and found a few guys rolling joints at a table. Feeling like veteran hash-heads, we approached the guys at the table and asked if we could buy some hash. These looked like the sort of guys my parents had always warned me about, but I hadn't noticed any respectable-looking gentlemen in pinstripe suits. They had loads of the stuff, and offered us a selection of ten pound deals. We decided what we wanted. They shared a few blasts of their joint with us, and we went off to a nearby table to roll our own joints.

When we got back on the dance floor we were stoned. Most of the guys had their tops off. I couldn't blame them. It was hot. Everyone was in lines across the dance floor, in rows like American Country & Western "line-dancing." The guys were stripped from the waist up. The girls wore running shorts and bras. All jumping to the pulsating sound of the music. Some of the girls looked incredibly beautiful. There were guys who wore fisherman hats and white gloves which glowed under the ultraviolet lights. These guys danced on the stage facing the crowd. I'd never seen such good dancers. The atmosphere at the rave was happy-go-lucky – everyone hugging each other.

The lights were brilliant, flashing strobes, moonbeams. We gyrated around the floor as the music thumped, the crowd jumped. We were out of our tree. Whistles blew in time to the music. The whole scene was just brilliant. Unfortunately I had to leave the rave at 11.30 p.m. because I'd promised Heidi that I'd be home by midnight. She didn't even know I was going to a rave. She thought I was just going to Stillorgan. As I left the pulsating atmosphere of the rave I said to myself, "Yeah, man, the hash and the rave . . . that's really the business . . . I'll be back!"

I spent the next few weeks singing the praises of the rave scene to my friends, and encouraged them to come to the next one. A new friend of mine, Gordon, said he'd come with me the next time. As we travelled into town on the bus he reminded me of myself on my first trip. He was shaking with excitement and, even though we didn't take stimulants at that particular rave, it was a great night. I had recruited another disciple.

Our next rave was far from innocent. I didn't know that it was about to change my entire life. I still can't believe how simply it all happened. Gordon and I went to the rave with little more on our minds than having some hash and enjoying the music. When we got there we felt the surge of music and smelt the old familiar aroma of hash, but suddenly something happened. We felt this strange curiosity about LSD – acid.

I suppose it went back a couple of weeks to when myself and a few friends – all girls – were on our way to a club. The girls met a few guys they knew, and they asked the girls if they'd like to do some acid. The girls were all eager to try some, but I wasn't really interested. I didn't have enough money with me anyway. But when we arrived at the club that night a dealer asked us if we wanted any acid, and the girls and the guys bought some. It was seven pounds a tab. A bit expensive for such a tiny piece of paper I thought. After about half an hour the girls started getting giddy. They were talking about the different objects they saw on each others faces. Weird, but I wanted to share their experience.

We leant against the balcony wall enjoying the sounds and watching the crowd on the dance floor. Gordon turned to me and said, "Would you be interested in doing some acid, Madzer?"

"Yeah, sure man, why not," I answered.

"Well, where do you think we could get some in here?" he asked.

"I suppose the only way is to go around and ask, just like we did when we got the hash here before," I replied.

We couldn't believe how easy it was. The very first person we asked said, "Yeah, sure, no problem, just stall for a few minutes and I'll be back." We hung around the same area dancing. Five minutes later the guy returned.

"They're Strawberries, lads. How many do you want?" he asked.

"How much are they?"

"Eight quid each," he said.

"We'll just take one." Gordon produced a tenner.

"Sound lads. Are you enjoying yourselves?" he asked in a flat Dublin accent.

"Yeah we sure are," I replied, as Gordon nodded.

"You'll enjoy yourselves a lot more when you take that . . . it's rapid!" he said.

The acid – and we'd spent eight pounds on it – was less than a quarter of an inch square! You could comfortably fit about six Strawberries on a standard postage stamp. The Strawberries look like a miniature transfer of a tiny strawberry on a plain yellow background. If you came across one in your child's bedroom, you'd think it was a tiny transfer for a toy or a model aeroplane! It was a major geometrical operation to divide the acid evenly into two pieces, but somehow we managed it. We put it on our tongues and chewed it around in our mouths for a while before swallowing it. It was the most unusual flavour I'd ever tasted in my life. A strong, sour acidic taste. We looked at each other and wondered, "What have we done?"

We danced for about twenty minutes. I noticed this strange light in the ceiling to my right, just below the balcony. It was the most interesting and fascinating light I'd ever seen. Truly amazing colours and shapes. I wondered why I hadn't seen this light before. Laser images beaming out a kaleidoscope of colours. I suddenly realised that it was the effect of the Acid. I turned to see how Gordon was getting on – he was dancing like a madman, eyes popping out of his head. I gave him a shove. He turned around – an enormous smile on his face – wild fiery eyes.

He shouted, "Look at the stage lights, Madzer, they're brilliant!" I didn't even reply. We headed for the gents toilets to get some water and take a leak.

We pushed and shoved our way through the crowd to the gents toilets where we were met by droves of wild-eyed characters, drenched in sweat, their tops off, wearing shorts. In the coolness of the gents toilets, Gordon and I lit a cigarette and had a few drags. The distortion was a lot more disturbing than seeing double when you're drunk. I looked at a place where the paint had peeled off the wall. As I looked, an image of a witch appeared. It was quite funny at the time.

Bright lights shone in the toilets. I looked at the faces going past and couldn't help noticing their eyes.

Their pupils were so dilated that I couldn't tell what colour they were. Some of them looked scary, almost devilish.

I went to have a leak. I looked down at my genitals. They had shrunk so much that I could hardly tell them from my fingers. I tried to focus. I began to wash my hands but I was in for another shock. My fingers were interlaced with each other in a knitting pattern. My hands were absolutely enormous. I hurried to the door of the gents to wait for Gordon. I took a few tokes from a joint offered to me by friends passing by. We made our way back to a couch at the side of the dance floor and exchanged notes. He couldn't believe how small his genitals had become either!

We spent the rest of the night dancing. The buzz was incredible. Gordon had this great big smile on his face and he couldn't get rid of it. At times we found ourselves sitting on the floor discussing such trivial things as the gel in our hair, or comparing our trainers with those of the other dancers. I didn't know then that most of the other people at the rave were on Ecstasy, not acid like Gordon and myself.

At about 2.00 a.m. we left the rave and walked as far as Donnybrook Bus Station where we hailed a taxi to take us home to Foxrock. The taxi ride was really strange. It felt as if we were travelling at hyperspeed up the dual carriageway with cars whizzing by us, leaving long red trails of light in their wake. Houses, bridges, garages and hotels moved and wobbled as we sped past them . . . as if they were being shaken by the draught from the car.

We didn't speak a word in the taxi. When we arrived at Foxrock Church we spent about half an hour waffling to each other about our experiences. We watched the cars flying by, put on our walkmans, and danced around the bus shelter. We must have looked like a pair of lunatics!

It must have been about 3.30 a.m. when we got back to Gordon's house and dug into a load of munchies . . . tea and toast. We went to the Shack, Gordon's converted garage. This Shack was some place . . . soft couches, armchairs, posters and exotic lighting, fully carpeted with a bed on a raised platform, and shelves filled with all makes of old beer bottles and cans. There was a good stereo system too. The Shack became a second home to us over the next months. Friends joined in our weekly expedition to the raves. They walked down Grafton Street, queued up to get into the rave, took some acid, and then came back to the Shack for munchies, music and waffle!

E FOR ECSTASY

The Shack was an ideal place for us to meet. Gordon's parents allowed him to have his friends there because it kept us out of the house and the insulation prevented the music from being a problem to the rest of the household. It was like our own little private detached apartment. It had its own entrance, so there was no need to go through the house. We had to take off our mucky shoes before we went into the Shack. That was Gordon's house-rule. I don't think Gordon's parents had a clue what was going on inside.

By now we had a pleasant group which met at the Shack regularly. We were joined by Danny, Peter, Eoin and Harry. Gordon was the self-appointed authority on dance music. Danny lived in a fantasy world about girls and would try to involve us in his imaginings. The fact that he'd only been out with one woman in his life might explain some of this. Peter was fascinated by every aspect of drugs. He wondered what was the biggest amount of hash he would see in his lifetime. He had a premonition that he would end up a junkie. Harry was always telling us about the various trips he'd experienced on acid. He'd end these stories with, "And that's why I'm giving it up." Eoin the joker, the movie star, loved to quote dialogue from films such as *The Shining*, *Mississippi Burning* and Robert De Niro classics.

Our weekends went something like this. We would meet at the Shack at around 7.30 p.m. on Saturday night. We'd have a few cans of beer, a few joints. We'd relax and listen to music, it was a warm-up for the rave. We'd wear jeans, runners, baggy sweats and jackets. An essential part of our kit was our rucksacks. My father used to wonder about my rucksack. He couldn't understand why I needed to bring such a thing to a dance. The rucksack contained Vick's vapour rub, a pair of socks, shorts, T-shirt, deodorant, walkman, towel and whistle. I'll explain this later. At about 8.30 p.m. we'd head off to get the bus into town, stopping at Newsrack on the way to buy some cigarettes and chewing gum. In town we'd walk down Grafton Street to McDonalds for some eats and drinks, and then we'd team up with some familiar faces from the previous weeks and make for the rave. I call them familiar faces because we never got to know their names, but we could always recognise the faces.

Inside the rave we found an alcove where we

changed into our shorts and T-shirts. We put our clothes into our rucksacks and left them in the cloakroom. We found a dealer who would sell us acid. We were seasoned druggies. We took our various drugs and got out onto the dance floor to mingle with the happy people.

The heat at these raves was absolutely incredible. I met a guy on one of my first visits to the rave . . . drenched in sweat as he came out of the gents toilets. Even if you dressed in shorts and didn't wear a top, the heat, the pace of the dancing, and the buzz of the crowd and the drugs made you sweat ferociously. People often collapsed on the floor from heat exhaustion and from the Ecstasy . . . the "Mad Bastards." Their mates would revive them. Onlookers would encourage them to inhale some more Vick's vapour rub, massage them and give them a few rushes.

Let me explain what these "rushes" are all about. Rushes are an uncontrolled blood flush surging through your body. When it happens, it gives a euphoric feeling. Rather like the adrenalin rush you get when you're under starter's orders in a race. The rush can be brought on by using energy. You put your arms straight up in the air over your head, get a friend to hold your hands and, as you try to force your hands down, he resists. As you continue to force your hands downwards, he will maintain strong resistance. When your hands eventually reach waist-level, having exerted every ounce of energy, he will suddenly withdraw the resistance. Immediately a tingling sensation surges through your body and gives you that "Ecstasy" feeling. Whenever I experienced this ecstatic feeling I realised how appropriately the drug was named. I went from hash to acid, and then eventually to Ecstasy over a period of about twelve months. Each substance has a different type of buzz. Hash is a mellow and relaxing buzz. It relaxed my whole body and made my head heavy. It made me very giddy and extremely sleepy. Acid and Ecstasy deaden your appetite. Hash increases your appetite. During some sessions, my friends and I would go through packets of rashers and sausages and loaves of bread washed down with mugs of tea. It was quite common during these "hash sessions" to drift off into a trance until someone would wake me up. Most people who use drugs probably start on hash and then progress.

The buzz from acid is completely different to the hash buzz. Acid enhances everything from touch to taste. It's a very lively buzz. It distorts your vision, and can give you some frightening hallucinations.

One time I came home, off my head on acid and, as I spoke with my dad, I saw he had three heads. "Oh no," I thought to myself . . . "how am I going to get through this one without him noticing?" I couldn't look him straight in the eyes because my pupils were dilated. The wallpaper whirled in a kaleidoscope. It was impossible to focus. My brain raced when I got into bed. I just wanted to close my eyes and go to sleep. But that didn't happen. As soon as I closed my eyes, the eyelid movie show started.

I decided to try Ecstasy. Harry and I met in our local pub/club one night, and we dropped down to another club nearby to buy a very special kind of Ecstasy, one called White Dove. We bought one White Dove for twenty pounds and returned to the comfort of our local club. We split the tab and took half a White Dove each, washed down with a pint because the taste of Ecstasy is absolutely putrid! Within fifteen minutes, I realised what everyone meant when they said that Ecstasy was the business. We were sitting at a table by the dance floor when suddenly I just had to get up on the floor and dance, dance, dance! Everyone in the club was my friend. The rushes through my body were electrifying, I smiled from ear to ear. The music was absolutely brilliant. I wanted to dance non-stop all night long.

Harry joined me on the floor but, unfortunately in his excitement and excessive smiling, he'd got lock-jaw! I thought it was terribly funny. This was our first real Ecstasy buzz. As we travelled home that night, we both agreed . . . Ecstasy . . . this really is the business.

The next morning I woke up feeling totally refreshed, vibrant and happy. I didn't know that I was still on the Ecstasy buzz from the night before! I thought that this was the wonder drug. The one for me . . . no side-effects, no hangover, loads of energy the next day. The perfect drug. If I'd known what was going to happen to me, I would never have touched that first White Dove. Peter and Eoin had already taken Mad Bastards (these were the original powerful Es, not the milder version that came on the market later). The whole group was now firmly switched on in a big way to Ecstasy – the designer drug of the nineties.

BIRTH, MARRIAGE AND DEATH

April 4th 1992 was the date set for my dad's marriage to Marina. To be quite honest, I felt apprehensive about the whole thing. My father's family had mixed feelings about the wedding. Heidi was against the match at first, but I think now that this was because she was worried about me. She couldn't understand it. "What does he think he's doing marrying a separated woman with three young children?" she asked me.

"I don't know," I replied.

"He finds it hard enough to manage you, let alone another three children. Does he know what type of responsibility he's taking on?" she said.

"I suppose he does, Heidi, sure he's met them and seen what they're like . . . little brats," I said.

"Sure you never know, Julian, this marriage may never happen . . . please God."

The drugs meant that I didn't know what I felt about anything. I was loyal to Heidi but I wanted to support my dad. I was afraid to say what I felt. Because I didn't know how I felt. I didn't want to even think about moving out of Monaloe and over to Rathfarnham where it was planned that we would live. I had plenty of friends living in my area, my school was behind my back garden. This marriage thing was a headache. I'd discussed this with my dad. I'd told him that I was in favour of the marriage. But, as the day approached, I began to get cold feet. Marina had three children. I'd met them and they got on my nerves. The eldest was only eleven years old, and I was seventeen! There was a wall between the three of them and me. I was in no hurry to climb it. The prospect of leaving Monaloe to live with these children horrified me. Monaloe was my first real home, where I'd made my first real friend, learnt to play football, had my first drink, and had my first kiss. It was my home, and I didn't want to leave it, my friends, or Heidi.

In March of 1992, just a month before the wedding day, Heidi brought me over to my Uncle Donal in Colchester in England. I talked with my Uncle Donal about the situation and he helped me to put things into perspective.

"Well, Julian, are you looking forward to the big day next month?" he asked.

"Yeah, I suppose so," I replied.

"What do you mean, you suppose so? Aren't you excited about it?" he queried.

"Well, Dad's asked me to be best man, and I don't know whether I want to do it or not," I said.

"Do you have a problem with being best man?" he asked.

"I don't know how the others will feel if I do it," I replied.

"What others?" he asked.

"Y'know, Heidi and the rest of the family. I don't

think they're too keen on the wedding anyway," I said.

"It doesn't matter what they think, Julian. What do you want to do?" he asked.

"I'd like to be best man, but I wouldn't fancy doing all those speeches and things," I said.

"I'm sure your dad can sort it out that you don't have to do all of those things. But how do you feel about the wedding itself?" he asked.

"I don't know. I've heard so many points of view that I don't know what my feelings are about it." I said.

"Do you think it's important to have a partner or a wife in this world, Julian?" he asked.

"Yeah, I do," I replied.

"Y'see, Julian, your father was married to your mother, but their marriage didn't work out. Since then it's just been yourself and your dad. Do you not think it would be nice for him to have a wife at this stage in his life . . . someone to be with when you're not around . . . someone to grow old with?" he asked.

"Yeah, you're right. It's a good thing that he's getting married. I hope it all works out well for him," I replied.

After our conversation I rang my dad and told him I'd be his best man – needless to say he was delighted.

"Dad, how are you? It's me . . . your long lost son," I said.

"How are things, Julian? How are you enjoying the holiday in Colchester?" he asked.

"Fine, I'm really enjoying myself. The shops are brilliant," I said.

"Tell Uncle Donal not to be spending all his money on you," he said.

"Remember you wanted me to be best man at your wedding, Dad?" I asked.

"Oh, the wedding. Yes, of course I remember," he laughed.

"Well, I've been thinking about it," I said.

"Well, that's a start, Julian," he said.

"I've decided to do it, to be your best man," I said.

"Brilliant, excellent, Julian. Good man," he said.

"But, Dad," I said.

"What, Julian?" he replied.

"I'm not making any speeches," I said.

"That's no problem, Julian. I can organise somebody to do MC at the wedding. The main thing is that you're going to be best man," he said.

"And, Dad," I said.

"Yes, Julian?" he replied.

"I'm going to be living with Heidi for the present, Dad," I said.

"Are you sure that's what you want to do?" he asked.

"Yeah, I've thought about it and I'd prefer to stay in Monaloe for the present," I said.

"Well, if that's what you want to do, that's OK. We can always review it further down the line?" he said.

"Yeah, sure. But is that OK with you?" I asked.

"Sure, that's great," he replied.

As I put down the phone, I sighed. What a relief to have all of that taken care of.

When I came back I knew the wedding would happen. I had convinced myself that it was for the best. I had agreed to be best man. My dad sorted out someone else to do MC at the wedding, which meant that I didn't have to make a speech. It was a testing time. It forced me to make a lot of decisions that I wouldn't have made otherwise. I was busy trying to keep everyone else happy. And I didn't even know how to make myself happy.

The day of the wedding arrived. We all headed up to Bangor on the evening before. I must explain that this was no simple uncomplicated wedding. Both Marina and my dad had been married before. They had both been divorced but, because there was no divorce in

Ireland, they couldn't remarry in the Republic of Ireland. On the Friday night in Bangor, Dad and I stayed in a friend's house. We checked the decorations in the church and made last minute arrangements. Great excitement. When we eventually retired to bed, we found it was a waterbed. I'd never slept in a waterbed before. It was really weird. Every time I moved my feet, my whole body would ripple. Dad was almost feeling sea-sick in it. We had a great laugh.

They had a civil wedding ceremony in the church in Bangor, Co. Down (Northern Ireland), followed by a small reception. It was originally meant to be soup and sandwiches for the guests who had travelled up from Dublin. But as we walked from the Chapel area into the function room, it suddenly became obvious that this was more than soup and sandwiches. There were all kinds of cakes, flans, cheesecakes, savouries and thousands of sandwiches. It was a magnificent spread. I couldn't get over the variety of strawberry flans, cream flans, pavlova cakes, meringues, chocolate cakes, etc. It was great to have Heidi there for the ceremony. She was the only one of Dad's family who travelled to Bangor.

Then we all travelled down to Dublin for the main reception, which was held in the cultural hall in the church. The meal and the speeches were just like any other wedding, except for the absence of alcoholic drink. Because it was a Mormon wedding reception there was no wine or champagne served, which meant a dry reception for those of us who enjoyed a drink. The church was beautifully decorated. But afterwards, as the enormous crowd of guests piled into the hall, it was totally different. Instead of the usual wedding band, they had a Country & Western band and a square-dance caller. This caller got almost everybody up on the floor doing all the American hoedown country dances. There was a great atmosphere in the place, but I wasn't too pushed about the reception. I wasn't really into the Country music and American thing, and I didn't know too many of the people. During the wedding I kept wondering how Heidi felt. Was she happy or sad, I wondered? Our side of the wedding were really quite stiff at first, and it took them some time to relax.

My Uncle Alan gave the speech about Marina, and to tell you the truth I wasn't too impressed. Marina's brother, Eugene, gave a speech about Dad, and it was only brilliant . . . really funny. I felt that Alan had let us down. My friend, Paul Hatton, had come to the wedding. If he hadn't been there I would have been bored, but because he was there we had a good laugh.

After the reception Dad and Marina flew out to Alberta in Canada on their honeymoon and to be sealed for time and all eternity in the Cardston Temple. My dad joined the Mormon Church in 1979 and he met Marina, who was also a member, in 1988. The civil marriage was "until death do us part," but, in the Church of Jesus Christ of Latter-Day Saints, the Temple sealing ceremony seals them together "for time and all eternity."

The first year flew by and, on 17th February 1993, little Jamie was born. I had expected a baby sometime, but not quite that soon. I felt quite good about the new arrival, even though a third half-sister added to my already complicated life.

"Congratulations, Marina. How are you feeling?" asked Heidi, as she gave Marina a kiss.

Marina was propped up on billowy white pillows. The whiteness of the pillows emphasised the darkness of the shadows under her eyes.

"Oh, I'm just a little bit tired," Marina replied.

"And well you should be," said Heidi.

I gave Marina a kiss too. I couldn't get over how

absolutely dreadful she looked. She seemed to have aged in a few days. I suppose that's what childbirth does to mothers. We all gathered around the cot.

"My goodness, look at the beautiful hair," said Heidi.

Little Jamie had a massive tuft of jet-black hair covering her head, and it stuck up in the front like a peaked cap.

"Oh, she's gorgeous, Marina," said Heidi, as she gently took her in her arms.

I could see the gentleness and the love in Heidi's eyes as she held little Jamie . . . she was a grandmother once more. As we sat around Marina's bedside admiring Jamie, there was a great sense of goodwill and happiness . . . all of us laughing and smiling together.

At the end of March, Heidi was taken into hospital with a persistent cough, a kind of flu. I moved over to Dad and Marina's in Rathfarnham because Heidi wouldn't like me staying in the house on my own. One night we had a function in the school – "the battle of the bands". Afterwards I invited close friends from school back to Heidi's house for a bit of a session. We had a few cans of beer and loads of hash. In fact we had a ball. Unfortunately I had to get back home to Rathfarnham to babysit for my dad and

Marina. As I left the house, I gave the lads instructions to tidy up everything, turn off all the lights and make sure the doors were locked when they left the house. Foolish me to think that I could trust them.

The next morning I woke up to the sound of a message being left on the telephone answering machine. My aunt had called into Heidi's house to check that everything was OK. The place was in a mess and, when she went upstairs, she found three strangers asleep in beds and on the floor! What a shock she got, and what a rumpus there was. How was I going to explain all this? My dad and I went over to Monaloe later that day to clean up the mess. The house wasn't too bad. But there were a lot of overflowing ashtrays lying around, and it wasn't the way Heidi would like it. The one place that was really trashed was my room. Bedsheets and duvet crumpled on the floor, cigarette butts everywhere, records lying around out of their sleeves, empty beer cans. Heidi would probably have freaked if she'd found out about it. I was angry with Harry and the others for letting it get into such a state but, in the end, it was my fault and no one else's. I didn't talk to my aunt or any of my uncles for ages after that. I knew what they were probably saying about me. If I got into any conversation they would surely pounce on me with the question "What did you think you were doing . . . have you no respect for Heidi's house?" This would then be followed by a lecture. I *hate* lectures.

Eventually everything was smoothed out, but it looked as if I would be living in Rathfarnham permanently from then on.

I was in sixth year in school. The pressure for the Leaving Certificate was beginning to build. The importance of the Leaving Cert. never really hit me. I was much more interested in my social life and my friends than studying, despite all the warnings and advice.

I will never forget that morning when I was sitting in class. A knock came to the door, and the secretary popped her head around the door and asked, "Is Julian Madigan here?"

"Yes," I replied.

"There's a telephone call for you in the office. It's your father," she said.

The secretary was in her fifties and, as we walked down the dimly lit corridor, she started telling me how her day had been so far.

"That stupid photocopier's broken again," she said.

I wondered why Dad had phoned me at school.

"It always happens on a day you really need it," she said.

"Sure, isn't it always the case," I said.

"Rushed off my feet as usual trying to get my reports done," she continued.

It must be important for Dad to ring me.

"It's a hard life. No rest," she concluded.

She pointed at the phone as we entered the office. It was almost covered with papers. I lifted the receiver and pressed the flashing button.

"Hello," I said.

"Hello, Julian," came the low sound of my dad's voice.

"I'm out here in the hospital, Julian . . . eh . . . " he faltered. I could tell that he was crying.

"Heidi was asking for you, Julian . . . eh . . . she was . . . " he faltered again.

"I think you should . . . come out to the hospital, Julian," he said.

"OK, Dad, I'll be straight out," I replied.

I was numb. Heidi must have died. I couldn't feel the phone in my hand. Somebody took it from me and replaced it. Ms Quirke looked at me with big questioning eyes.

"My grandmother's dead," I said to Ms Quirke as the tears flowed down my cheeks. Those three words were the hardest words I've ever had to say.

"I'm so sorry," Ms Quirke replied.

I wanted to run out of the school, as far away as possible, and just sit in a large open field and cry. The principal came in. He wasn't my favourite person.

"I'm so sorry about your grandmother's death, Julian. She was such a lovely woman," he said.

I felt like standing up and hitting him. Ms Quirke brought me to the hospital. My father was waiting for me as I got out of the car. Ms Quirke immediately expressed her condolences to Dad, but he said, "My mother hasn't died. She's very close to the end, and I thought that Julian should see her before she lapses into unconsciousness again."

"She's not dead?" I said.

"No . . . she's not dead, Julian," he said.

"But I thought you said . . . "

"No, you must have misunderstood me," he said.

"Well how is she?" I asked.

"She's very weak, and the doctors don't know whether she'll last through the day. She was asking for you earlier on, so I thought you should be here when she regains consciousness."

The sense of relief was unbelievable.

We spent the next two days going in and out of the hospital in Loughlinstown visiting Heidi. It was heartbreaking to watch her lying in the bed with an oxygen mask on her face, barely breathing. She looked frail and old, almost lifeless. Her mother, my great-grandmother, had died in 1988 at 101 years of age. Heidi, with her gaunt face and sunken eyes, now looked the image of her mother. She lay there, propped up on pillows, with an intravenous drip in her arm, a tube inserted in her back, looking like death and barely breathing. This wasn't the enthusiastic and young-at-heart Heidi that I had been living with all these years. Not the woman who had cared for me, who would have sacrificed anything for my happiness. A mother to me. She was the kindest and most loving person I had ever known. It would never cross her mind that I would come back from school to find an empty house. She was there, with food prepared and a warm welcome. Heidi in the hospital was a like a ghost.

On Friday 24th April 1993 we were all in the hospital around lunch-time. Heidi lapsed in and out of consciousness. I was supposed to run a race in Belfield that afternoon. I talked to Heidi, even though she could only respond with slight nods. I promised her I was going to win a medal for her when I ran my race that afternoon. She smiled. She tried to squeeze my hand, and then I went off to run my race. I *did* win a medal in the race, but, when I returned to the hospital she had deteriorated. I tried to show her the medal and tell her that I had won it for her, but she couldn't hear me. The doctors said that this could go on for another day or two. My dad suggested that I go off to Paul Hatton's house for the rest of the afternoon. He would collect me there later. Paul had been my constant companion for the past days. He lived on the same estate, and he was very fond of Heidi. He was one of the friends I know who has never touched drugs in any shape or form.

At 6.30 p.m. that day, when Paul and I were watching a video in his house, a knock came to the door. Paul told me it was my dad. Dad was standing at the door with a lost, almost speechless look on his face. Motionless. I knew immediately that Heidi had died. The emptiness that came over me was like nothing I'd ever felt. Someone had just ripped out my entire stomach.

Difficult days followed. When we went to the morgue at the hospital I couldn't look at her lying there in a coffin. That wasn't how I wanted to remember her. I walked down towards the dual carriageway. As I stood there alone I thought of Heidi and burst into tears. One of my relatives came up beside me and told me that Heidi wouldn't like to see me crying . . . it was true.

The day of the funeral was a bombshell. The final laying to rest tore me apart, the knowledge that this was indeed the end . . . she would never be around for me again. The church was packed to capacity and, when we arrived at Deansgrange cemetery, there were hundreds of relations and friends gathered around the graveside.

As the coffin was lowered into the ground, the sun glinted on the handles of the coffin. As the first shovel of earth was thrown on top of the casket, I had to be literally dragged from the graveside. This really was the end. It was as if my blood had been sucked from my veins. My spirit had left me, because that's what Heidi was . . . my life and soul, my rescuer. I felt so lonely, so cheated by life. I thought of all the things she had done for me, and there was no way now that I could pay her back. I looked at the coffin and thought about all the good times that we'd had together. The fun, the laughter, and the silly arguments which would often end with, "I'm never speaking to you again." But in five minutes we would be joking about something else.

Heidi was gone. The woman who would stay awake at night until she heard the door close behind me, and knew that I was home safe. The person who would always show love and affection for me, no matter what I did.

I don't know how I would have got through that ordeal without my friend Paul. But nothing could comfort me. Life would never be the same again. Through all the ups and downs in my life, my parents' separation, moving houses and changing schools, Heidi had always been there.

THE NEW YEAR'S EVE TRIP

Christmas was always a very happy time for me. Monaloe on Christmas Day was magic. The peace, the warmth, the excitement of giving and receiving presents. The surprise as presents were opened. We never moved out of the house on Christmas Day except for the traditional walk around the block in the evening after Christmas dinner.

It was a tradition that we'd receive visitors for smoked salmon, pâté and drinks from about 10.30 in the morning until about 2.00 in the afternoon. Then the family, Heidi with her five children, and their spouses and children, would settle down to a wonderful Christmas dinner. A blazing fire, the

Christmas tree lit up in the corner, holly and Christmas decorations, Christmas crackers, balloons, and plenty of toys and games strewn about the place. There were always young children around at Christmas time. There was a great "one big happy family" feeling.

The Christmas of 1993 was different. Heidi died in April of that year. Without the normal family gathering in Monaloe, Christmas was empty. The house in Monaloe had been sold. I'd gone to live with my father and my stepmother in Rathfarnham. I was living with two stepbrothers and a stepsister, and a new baby half-sister. Yes, Christmas of 1993 was different. There was the same excitement from Marina's children about the toys. It reminded me of early days in Monaloe. A feeling of joy as presents were exchanged. But it was different. Strange to live in a household as one of five children, when I'd been an only child for seventeen years!

New Year's Eve of 1993 will always stick in my mind because of the crazy things that happened on that long and eventful evening. As far back as I can remember, we celebrated New Year's Eve as a family. We played Monopoly until the stroke of midnight, then rang in the New Year with champagne, Auld Lang Syne, etc.

The biggest night of the year. The whole group decided to celebrate together in the local pub/club. We arrived at the club at about 6.00 p.m. We had to be there early enough to get the right seats downstairs by the dance floor. We sat around the table for a while as the place began to fill up. And we were approached by a man who dealt acid and Ecstasy regularly.

"Do you want any acid?" he asked in a sarcastic tone of voice.

"Yeah, give us a 100," I replied. We laughed. I asked him what kind of acid he had.

"Microdots," he replied, and immediately I looked at Harry and suggested that we did some acid.

"We've got Strawberries . . . what about a swap of two Strawberries for two Microdots?" I suggested.

"Yeah, fine. Follow us into the jacks and we'll talk business," he said with a smile. I followed him into the toilets a few moments later. There was quite a queue outside one of the cubicles. People who wanted to do business with him. The cubicle door opened. Out popped his head and he called me in.

"I'll do that swap, but you'll have to give me four quid during the night because I'm selling these for seven quid each and I paid over three quid for them. Is that OK?" he asked.

"Yeah, that's cool," I said, and we swapped Strawberries for Microdots.

By 8.30 p.m. we'd sold twenty of our Strawberries to friends in the club. Harry and I pushed our way over towards the bar to buy two pints, and then we sat down and popped the Microdots. The Microdots were wrapped in tinfoil and it was difficult to unwrap them because of their size. They're about the same size as the tip of a ballpoint pen, absolutely tiny but very potent. I thought Strawberries were small – but Microdots were tiny. You could fit about ten of these on a postage stamp. It's a more mescaline-based drug than acid. More intense. It brings you further into the trip than acid does.

The place was packed to capacity by the time we took the Microdots. Harry and I got separated in the crowd. It didn't matter, we were both on a high. The trip got heavier, which is what I expected, but the visuals that came along with it were something else, something that I'd never expected. I looked out on the dance floor, at the people dancing. Their legs and arms were helicopter blades, whirling around. Faces made of jelly, distorted. I was disoriented. I couldn't identify with the rest of the group because they were on Ecstasy or speed – not my kind of buzz that night . . . I was on an acid trip. Harry was lost in the crowd. Suddenly I just had to get out of the place.

I pushed and shoved my way through the crowd

and drank in the fresh air outside. I went over to a wall opposite the club and sat down. The doors closed and I thought to myself, "I'll never get back in now to ring in the New Year." But then I realised it wasn't important. I hadn't got my head together yet.

I decided to go for a walk around town to clear my head. As I reached the top of Dawson Street, the church bells started to ring out. The bells seemed to be ringing at different intervals, no synchronisation. My head was in the middle of a quadraphonic sound system. I was surprised that I couldn't actually see the bells. I thought to myself, "If this is the state I'm in now, this is going to be some crazy year!" Little did I know how crazy it was going to be. By the time I returned about half an hour later, the doors were open again. My head was a little bit clearer and the visuals had subsided considerably.

At about 3.00 a.m. the music stopped and the lights came on. What a spectacle! I couldn't believe there were so many people in the place, the railing on the stairs had collapsed during the night. I looked at them falling around the place, drunk, stoned and E'd. Or tripped out of their heads. Funny to watch the "where am I? . . . what's happening? . . . who are you?" expressions on the faces.

We regrouped and went off in search of a taxi to

bring us to Harry's house. We were going to sleep there that night because his parents were away. We stalled for a few minutes outside the club to roll a couple of joints for the journey, and then made our way to Nassau Street for our taxi out to Blackrock. At about 4.00 a.m. we arrived at Harry's house and started making cups of tea in the kitchen. We rolled joints from a large stash of hash as we sat around the large wooden table, still high on Microdots. The intensity of the Microdot was incredible. Eight hours after taking it, and the buzz was as strong as if we'd just taken a Strawberry. We had another half Strawberry each to welcome in the New Year. We discussed the trips we'd been on that night, and Eoin entertained us with his renditions of Jack Nicholson from *The Shining*, and Robert De Niro from *Cape Fear*.

The crack was absolutely mighty, except for one flaw . . . Harry had a bad trip. We noticed that he had been missing for a while and, when we found him, he was in the front room crying. Peter tried to talk him round and get his head together with a few joints. I don't know what Harry went through on that bad trip but, when he came back he wasn't himself. I talked with him later and knew he was different . . . he had changed. To tell you the truth, I don't think he was ever the same again.

CHAPTER FOUR

THE BUSINESS ANGLE

My habit was costing a lot of money, and I began to
think about ways of getting cash. I'd already done a
small bit of "dealing." I supplied some friends and
acquaintances. Never anything major, just a few short
runs. I was paid in hash – enough to roll a few joints.
Drugs weren't helping my school work. I'd just failed
my Leaving Certificate in my local school. I was now
living permanently with Dad and Marina in
Rathfarnham, and, although I knew he was
disappointed, he didn't make a huge issue of it at the
time. I think he knew how upset I was about Heidi's
death. But I needed my Leaving so I enrolled in
another school, outside my own area.

My dad was totally against this, he felt that I

should go and work for a couple of years before trying to concentrate on studies again. He believed that I was not in "study mode," as he put it and, until such time as I was ready for study, it was a waste of time going to school again.

"Julian, I can't understand why you want to repeat the exam. You had every opportunity to study for it, you told me that you were studying for it, and now you've failed it. Why do you think it will be different this time around?" asked Dad.

"Dad, you know how disruptive the past year has been. It was impossible to concentrate on any sort of serious study. Now I'm ready to get down to serious study," I said.

"You're a long way from ready, Julian. Has your conduct changed in any way since you sat the examination?" he asked.

"Not really, but I'm ready to change now," I said.

"Julian, you're not switched on to 'study mode' right now. You need to get out into the world and work for a couple of years in order to appreciate the importance of studying and learning," he said.

"I do appreciate the importance of it. I will get down to serious study this year," I pleaded.

"Julian, I think you're crazy to enrol in another school. You're going to waste another year of your life. However, if you think that you can change that much . . . fine. But I'll be keeping a close eye on your study patterns and your class attendance," he said.

This was in the autumn of 1994. I made a lot of friends at my new school. We had one thing in common . . . most of us were druggies! One of the guys, Mick, was dealing quite a lot of hash in the school. It wasn't difficult to see what type of money he was making. He went to his dealer on Thursday with wads of twenty pound notes, and came back with large quantities of hash which he sold to the students at school. He smoked a lot of hash in the school. He had this saying – "the finest deals in Dublin." I thought I'd make a lot of money if I could score some acid to deal in school.

I asked around – outside school. Did anyone know anyone who would supply me with some acid. A friend, Eithne, told me about a friend of hers who would be able to sort me out with anything I wanted. I arranged a meeting with this individual who was named Francie. He set up a drop-off point in Dawson Lane, the alley that links Dawson Street with South Frederick Street.

I waited in the alley feeling nervous. This was the first time I'd ever tried anything like this. Francie arrived with his girlfriend at about 9.00 p.m., and dropped a packet of one hundred tabs of acid at my feet.

"All right man, how's it going . . . sorry about being a bit late," he said in his deep Dublin accent.

"No worries, it's cool," I replied.

"There's a hundred acid in that packet. They're Strawberries . . . is that all right?" asked Francie.

"Yeah, that's OK, in fact that's what I was hoping to get," I said.

"Be careful when you're selling that, and watch where you go . . . look out for the cops," he warned.

"Yeah, I'll be fine. I'm really just selling them to some friends in school," I replied.

"If you get caught by the cops, don't mention a word about me. Tell them you got them off some guy in Oliver Bond flats because, if you squeal on me and I get caught, your life won't be worth living. OK?" he said.

"Fine, no need to worry, I won't say a word." I began to wonder what on earth I was getting myself into . . . this was a dangerous business.

"They're two quid each, so that means you owe me two hundred quid, but there's no rush with the money. Get it to me as soon as you sell enough to make the two hundred quid . . . all right?" he said.

"Yeah, that's OK. As soon as I have the money I'll

get in contact with Eithne and she'll contact you. Is that OK?" I asked.

"Fine. Just be careful . . . see you around." He and his girlfriend headed off in the direction of Dawson Street.

I put the one hundred acid tabs into the breast pocket of my jacket and then I went straight to my local pub to meet Eithne.

I had the acid. I hadn't had to fork out two hundred quid to get it. I felt that this was an opportunity to earn some much needed extra cash to spend at the weekends, buy some clothes and generally live it up. But actually shifting the stuff among friends was a different ball game. Harry and I used to sell it to our friends at school and in some of the clubs.

It was usually quite easy to ply our trade in the local pub/club without any interference from the management but I was very nearly caught red-handed once. I'd just finished a deal when I suddenly noticed that I was being surrounded on all sides by management types. I was standing on the balcony. Three bouncers were coming up the stairs. The manager of the club was approaching from the only other balcony exit, followed closely by two more bouncers. "This is it," I thought, as I racked my brains for some good reason why I should have about forty acid tabs. Let me explain. The 40 acid tabs were on a sheet about the size of two regular postage stamps. forty tiny pictures of strawberries that could be easily mistaken for miniature colour transfers.

"What are those things in your hand?" asked the manager in a curious tone of voice.

"They're mine." I stalled for time.

"Yes, I gathered that, but what are they?" he persisted.

"They're little pictures of strawberries," I answered, trying to sound innocent as I handed them to him. He took them and looked at them, mystified.

"And what do you do with these might I ask?" he enquired.

"I'm a student at the College of Art and Design, and I use these as additions to my pictures. My friend makes them for me in his print shop." I was making up the story as I was telling it.

"Why are they wrapped in tinfoil?" he asked.

"My friend just made them for me this evening and dropped them in to me here at the club. So I wrapped them in tinfoil because the print isn't completely dry on them yet."

I noticed that Harry was standing about ten feet away from us rolling a three-skinner joint, which we'd planned to share before I was accosted by the management "A Team squad!" Suddenly one of the bouncers realised what was happening. He grabbed the three-skinner from Harry and shouted to the manager, "Sure look what this guy's doing over here." He had a triumphant grin on his face, but it disappeared when he examined the contents of the three-skinner and found that it contained only tobacco.

I looked over at Harry and found it hard to hide a smile as he lit up the three-skinner. This little incident took the tension out of things. But the manager handed me back my "works of art" and said, "You're very lucky . . . other managers of other establishments wouldn't be as understanding as I am." He hadn't been conned by my story.

SPRING OF '94

Around the middle of January '94, we decided that we should try to give up acid. We'd found ourselves doing acid in the Shack and the parks around our area. We no longer went into the clubs or even into town. Our main rave club had closed down, so we didn't have a place to do our thing. We also realised that acid was causing us all problems because we were so disoriented that we forgot to do things, go places, keep appointments, etc. We were all in permanent trouble with our parents.

We decided that hash was the lesser of two evils (not that we considered either to be evil at this stage). Hash didn't wreck your head the way acid did, you could take small amounts at a time, and it was a more sociable drug . . . like alcohol. It was a natural plant and should be less harmful to us than acid, which was a chemical. Around this time there was a decline in our Ecstasy intake because none of us could afford it. We had no income, so it was a great treat when we got the chance to do it occasionally. I soon gave it up because I had no real interest in the club scene at this time.

It was also possible to get a great trip out of hash simply by smoking a large amount of the stuff, or by doing "buckets", "waterfalls" and "hot knives." These were the various ways of increasing the intensity of the hash with the use of empty plastic cider bottles and buckets of water. I won't go into the details of exactly how these were accomplished, but it's just like getting super value for the same amount of hash . . . 50% extra FREE!

It makes me laugh now when I hear people say

that hash is quite harmless because it's a natural plant with no physically addictive properties. Within a month, every one of us needed a joint every day. The dependency grew as the weeks went by. It became impossible to stay at home for any length of time without a powerful urge to be off with my mates enjoying a joint. During the week, it was just a daily fix, but we smoked constantly at the weekends. We drank and listened to music in the Shack, or some other place where we could sit down and enjoy the hash away from our parents. We were all confirmed hash-heads.

One weekend myself and my girlfriend Tina decided to go into town again to check out a new club. I'd heard a lot about this club since it opened at the beginning of the year and when I arrived there I wasn't disappointed. There was a long queue outside. The doors were manned by the usual four bouncers in black. As you went in you were searched. This whole searching exercise is an absolute joke. No matter how carefully they search you, it's easy to hide vast quantities of acid and E in jacket linings, belts, shoes and all sorts of places. The only effective search would be a strip-search.

This club was really good, the music was brilliant, the atmosphere was superb. E was available at every corner. After being there for a few weekends in a row, I thought it was time to go back to the old designer drug again. So I bought some E from a friend of mine and boy! did the place start to kick. From then on we changed from hash bashes to E parties. The group started to frequent this new dance club in town.

The E habit was far more expensive than hash. We badly needed some way of making money . . . like a job! We all got jobs. I got a nice job in town close to my E supply. The dealer who supplied me lived only five minutes away from where I worked. Our weekends on E lengthened. Instead of doing acid or E on a Saturday night, we started on Friday nights after work. On Thursdays we bought supplies of E for the weekend. On Friday nights we did E in the Lodge. On Saturday nights we headed for the new dance club in town. On Sundays we came down by getting stoned or drunk, or sometimes both . . . what a life!

The problem with doing E was that you needed hash to bring you down. Imagine being on top of the world for about three hours, and then being brought down to earth with a bang! Well that's what happens when you do E without the cushioning effect of a few nice joints at the end of it.

One morning when I was at work I got a phone call from my dad who said he would meet me for lunch at 1.00 p.m. It sounded quite important. I met him as arranged.

We sat down to have some salad rolls on a bench by the canal, and suddenly he hit me with a bombshell.

"Did you know that Harry has been convicted and sent to St Patrick's Institution for young offenders?" I nearly swallowed my roll.

"He's what?" I replied.

"Do you realise how serious this is, Julian?" he asked.

"Of course I do," I replied.

"I thought Harry was fairly straight, but obviously he's as bad as those other weirdos you've been hanging around with," he said.

"Harry is OK, Dad. I can't understand how this happened," I said.

"Have you been seeing Peter or Danny recently?" he asked.

"No, I told you I was avoiding them," I lied.

"Well you'll need to be very careful about your involvement with Harry too, Julian. Whatever he's into can incriminate you by association," he said.

"What did his parents say?" I asked.

"They don't even know yet, Julian," he said.

"How did you find out?" I asked.

"A priest from St Patrick's Institution rang me. Harry had given him your number, so the priest called me. And that's the sad thing about it. I tried to contact Harry's parents but they're on holiday somewhere down the country. I was able to contact his brother, Michael, so he'll get in touch with them. Are you sure you're not in any trouble, Julian?" he asked.

"Positive, Dad," I replied.

I hadn't a clue what had happened to Harry, but I was hoping it was nothing to do with drugs. The first people I needed to contact were Peter and Danny to find out what happened.

By the end of the summer in '94 I found myself divided between three different groups of people. My friends were all drug abusers because, now that I was doing E on a regular basis, I didn't have anything in common with straight people. The original group was still intact. We had our regular meetings in the Shack. But I was becoming drawn towards another group in the Stillorgan area who were into drugs and late night parties. The weekly routine was slightly different with this group. We didn't go into town to do our E.

Instead, we had parties every night of the weekend in somebody's house. We started doing E at about 9.00 p.m. when we arrived at the party. The party would go on until about six the following morning. It all depended on whether the parents came home. My weekends stretched. The parties started on Thursday night, which meant the weekend went from Thursday night until Sunday evening, sometimes ending on Monday at 6.00 a.m. This caused trouble at home. My dad tried to find out where I was, who I was with, where I stayed over, etc. I had to think up reasonably credible excuses.

"Where were you until this hour, Julian?" came my dad's voice from the top of stairs, as I was gently closing the door behind me at five o'clock on a Monday morning.

"Hi, Dad. What are you doing up at this hour?" I replied.

"Waiting for you to come home, Julian. Where were you?" he asked again, as he started down the stairs. This meant it was going to be one of those interrogation sessions . . . who, where, why, when, etc.

"Did you not say that you'd be home on the last bus from town on Saturday night?" he asked.

"Yes, I did, but we missed the last bus, and we all got a taxi to Harry's house," I said.

It was fairly safe to mention Harry's. When he got out of St Patrick's he met my dad and convinced him that he had learnt his lesson and was turning over a new leaf.

"So you all stayed over in Harry's house last night?" he asked.

"No, only three of us stayed with Harry, and the others walked home to Foxrock," I said.

"Then why didn't you ring me and let me know where you were?" he said.

"I didn't want to wake you at that hour of the morning. We didn't get back to Harry's until after three o'clock," I explained.

"I'm not talking about Saturday night, Julian, I'm talking about all day Sunday. Why didn't you ring to let me know that you'd stayed in Harry's house?" he asked.

"I thought I'd be home during Sunday afternoon, but nobody called us and we slept it out until six o'clock in the evening," I said.

"And what did you do from six o'clock until now, which is ten past five?" he asked.

"We had something to eat in Harry's, and then we just went into town," I explained.

"Until five in the morning!" he said.

"We missed the last bus home . . . "

"Oh, missed the last bus home again, is it? Was Eoin staying over in Harry's with you?" he suddenly asked.

"Yes," I said.

"Isn't that amazing, Julian, because I was talking to his father today, and he said that Eoin was home at midnight last night."

How do I get out of this one, I thought to myself.

"Well, maybe he did, but I thought he came back in the taxi with us. Oh no, that's right, we dropped him at Temple Hill and he said he was going to walk home. But he couldn't have been home at midnight," I said.

"Well I'm sick and tired of ringing around and wondering where you are at weekends. In future I need to know exactly where you're going, precisely who you're going with, and you'll be home here at a reasonable hour. I'm not having any more sleepless nights worrying about you," he said.

"OK, Dad . . . I'm sorry," I said.

I was rapidly running out of excuses. There can only be so many twenty-first birthday parties, so many going-away parties, end-of-job parties, welcome-home parties. My dad used to ring people's houses in the early hours of the morning asking where I was. This was embarrassing to say the least. But I didn't want to stop doing E so I kept going to the parties and my excuses became more and more elaborate.

The third group I got involved with were male and female "happy people" – about thirty of them – who used to meet almost every night at Murphys' house in Monkstown. The Murphy parents lived abroad and their children had the freedom of the house. They ranged in ages from eighteen to twenty-four, and they knew everybody and anybody. There was always a great buzz in Murphys'. The house was a large detached bungalow with a small garden. It had two large bay-windows on either side of the front door. There was a tiny kitchen at the end of the long hallway, but we spent most of our time in the dining-room or television room. You could tell that parents weren't there. The house was always untidy, especially the kitchen where the bins were always overflowing.

During the week I'd drop into Murphys' for a few joints and listen to some music and meet with the gang. But at weekends it was non-stop E all the way. There would always be a party somewhere. Sometimes we'd all go into town to one of the clubs.

Somebody in the gang was bound to have been invited to a party afterwards and we'd all go with him. There was a great happy family buzz about the Murphy gang. The common denominator was E, hash and acid. Our weekends nearly always finished in Murphys'.

I was doing E all the time. I needed more cash. When I started on E one tablet at a time was enough for a good buzz. But now I needed three or four a night. The tablets cost about fifteen pounds each, plus the cost of hash and speed, plus bus fares, taxis, and admission to clubs. It was all very expensive. The people in the three groups, the Shack group, the Stillorgan group, and Murphys' gang all came from affluent areas like Stillorgan, Foxrock, Deansgrange, Blackrock and Cabinteely. Money wasn't a problem to some of them. But it was a problem for the rest of us. We began to talk about dealing again as a way of feeding the habit.

A few of the guys in Stillorgan were already dealing. So were some of the guys in Murphys' group. Peter, Danny and myself from the Shack gang started doing a few deals. At first it was messy and a lot of the deals fell through but we started to deal with Jacko from the Stillorgan gang, and things went quite smoothly. Then Danny and Peter tried to pull a fast one on me by delaying payments on Es. I couldn't possibly meet Jacko and have no money for him. As the days passed I realised that I would be short some of the money, just how much I didn't know. After doing my figures, I realised that I was owed £300 by various people. These people were unreliable when it came to paying debts. I met Jacko, and he wasn't pleased. I ended up having a fight with him, and came out of it with a bloody nose.

"What do you mean they didn't come up with the money they owed you, Madzer?" said Jacko.

"They've been avoiding me, Jacko. I've been ringing their houses and calling around to them, but they're messing me about," I said.

"I told you when I gave you the stuff, Madzer, it's cash on delivery. If they haven't got the money, hit them! They'll soon come up with it," he said.

"Yeah, but when you can't even get to them, Jacko . . . " I started.

Whack! Suddenly I was holding my nose as the blood gushed out.

"What the hell was that for?" I said.

"That's what you should have given them, Madzer, and then you wouldn't be holding your nose," said Jacko.

I was more annoyed at Peter and Danny than I

was with Jacko. I felt that Jacko was right to do what he did because it was his ass on the line. Sure I didn't even try to hit back or defend myself. Stupid thinking or what?

"You better have that £300 on Wednesday, Madzer, or I'm telling you . . . your life won't be worth living," said Jacko.

"I'll have it. Don't worry. Danny and Peter are just late giving me the money they owe me," I said.

The next day I knew I couldn't wait for Danny or Peter to pay up, and somehow I needed to get my hands on £300 fast.

Father Desmond was the Chaplain of my old school. He was also a good friend. I rang him and told him that I was in a spot of bother. Could I meet him? We met that evening, and I explained that I owed £300 to a dodgey character.

"Y'see, I owe him the money since the summer when I asked him for a loan," I explained.

"And who is he?" said Father Desmond.

"A friend of a friend," I explained.

"Is he involved with criminals?" said Father Desmond.

"I don't know. Maybe he is," I said.

"I'll see what I can do, but I can't promise you anything, Julian," he said.

"OK. I'm really sorry for asking, but you were the only person I could think of," I said.

"Not to worry. I'll ring you in the morning. I'll see what I can do," he said.

I met him in Deansgrange the next morning, and he had the money for me. I promised him the money back within four months, with interest.

"Don't worry about the interest. But you should stop hanging around with those types of people, they're no good for you, and they'll only drag you down."

I left Father Desmond and went straight to Jacko with the money. That was the last I saw of Father Desmond.

My next step was to hunt down Danny and Peter. I met them the next day in Cornelscourt, and told them about the trouble they'd got me into. But they didn't care. Eventually, after constant nagging, they paid me the money. There is no honour among thieves, and our little cartel dissolved fairly soon after it started.

I started working in McDonalds in Blackrock to earn some money and, although the work was hard, I was enthusiastic and the rest of the staff were great. It gave me a bit of cash to buy drugs, and I began to do some very small deals myself for a while. However, the whole drugs thing really came to a head one night after finishing work in McDonalds.

My dad collected me from work at about 11.00 p.m. We had barely arrived home. I was sitting in the front room talking to Marina and my dad when the front doorbell rang. Dad went out to answer the door and next second I heard a voice coming from the front door, "Is Julian Madigan here?" Suddenly this large man was standing over me showing me his identification. He was a member of the Dublin Drug Squad. "Are you Julian Madigan?" he asked.

"Yes," I replied. I watched the expressions of shock and horror on Marina's and Dad's faces.

"Stand up," he growled. His partner pinned my arms behind my back and asked, "Where is your bedroom?"

"Upstairs," I replied as they marched me out of the room. I thought to myself . . . this must be a joke. As they took me out of the front room towards the stairs, a third guy, a garda dressed in a suit and tie, stood at the doorway and held a search-warrant in front of my face to show me that this was for real. My two stepbrothers and stepsister heard the commotion and stood trembling outside their bedroom doors, eyes aghast, mouths open, as the two men bundled me into my bedroom. I knew this was for real . . . this was a drugs bust! The third man was downstairs showing Marina and Dad the search-warrant.

"Take off your clothes," said the first man.

"All of them?" I enquired.

"Yes, all of them. You heard what I said," he replied. As I took my clothes off they searched the room and kept asking me questions.

"So where is it . . . where have you hidden it . . . we know you have it," they kept saying to me.

"I don't know what you're talking about . . . I don't have anything."

I realised that there were two types of character to be reckoned with here . . . a good guy and a bad guy. The good guy was going through the routine, but I was really afraid of the bad guy, afraid that he was going to break my arms or something. When I was stripped to my underpants, they examined my arms and legs for needle marks.

"What do you use these for?" Good Guy enquired when he found the various knives that I'd collected.

"Nothing really, just for show. They're knives that I've picked up over the years," I said.

They searched the room meticulously, took out my clothes and examined them, emptied my drawers, checked under the corners of the carpet.

"Your hair looks quite natural, doesn't it?" said Good Guy.

"Yeah, very natural," laughed Bad Guy.

I'd just had my hair dyed a platinum blond colour that week.

"Where were you last Thursday?" Bad Guy asked.

I tried to gather my thoughts.

One of them said, "We know where you were. You were in Cornelscourt and then you went down to Deansgrange." My mouth dropped open in amazement. They must have been following me for a while.

"What do you use these for . . . I suppose they're for doing cocaine?" Bad Guy quizzed me when they found some small mirrors in the room.

"No they're not. That's just talcum powder on them. I keep them in my toilet bag," I replied.

"What's this?" Good Guy showed me a polythene bag with a year-old magic mushroom in it.

"That's a dead magic mushroom . . . it's there over a year," I said.

"If there's anything here you might as well tell us now because we'll find it . . . we'll bring in the dogs if we have to," said Bad Guy. I knew that there was nothing in the house. But I was worried when they mentioned the dogs. Crumbs of hash must surely be ingrained in the carpet.

Bad Guy left, but Good Guy stayed to talk to me.

"What are you doing with your life? You're wasting it away," he said.

I just listened.

"The crowd you're with are just a pack of no-good wasters. They're losers, Julian. Are you happy? What do you think your parents think, having a druggie for a son?" he asked.

I didn't say anything. This was all just too much. How did they know about me? Who put them on to me? What was I going to tell Dad?

"You'd want to stop hanging around with those so-called friends, and start cleaning up your act. We're going to keep an eye on you, Julian, from now on," he said. He left the room. I was in a state of shock and, to be honest with you, I didn't know what to feel, or how to react. All I knew was that my house had just been raided by the Drug Squad.

My dad came upstairs when they had gone.

"Well, what was all of that about, Julian?" he asked.

"To tell you the truth, Dad, I don't know," I said.

"What do you mean you don't know? They had a search-warrant," he said.

"Someone must have given them my name, to get

them off their backs. That's the only explanation I have for it," I said.

"Are you doing drugs?" asked Dad.

"I smoke a small bit of hash, that's all, Dad," I said.

"What about your friends then?" he asked.

"Yeah, some of them dabble in it. Nothing hard or anything," I said.

"Are you telling me that Peter doesn't take drugs?" he asked.

"He takes a bit of hash as well," I said.

"Well I happen to know, Julian, that both Peter and Danny are both heavily into drugs . . . acid and Ecstasy. What have you got to say about that?" he asked.

"I don't know what they do in their own time," I replied.

"I don't think Harry is as reformed as he says he is, and Peter has been in Coolmine for drug treatment, Julian. Are you telling me that you didn't know about that?" he asked.

I didn't say a word. After a few minutes silence the conversation began again at a more relaxed and gentle pace. One of the reasons for it being so relaxed was that my dad was sitting in the big armchair which I had in the corner of my room. I called it the "smoker's throne."

"Julian, you've no idea how serious this is. I've been in the music business for about fifteen years. I've seen guys get hooked on drugs of one sort or another. Some of those guys are now dead. Others are going to spend the rest of their lives in places like St John of God's. That's not living, Julian . . . that's only existing. Surely that's not what you want to look forward to? It doesn't matter whether it's alcohol, nicotine, hash, Ecstasy or cocaine, they all get a grip on you unless you do something about it."

"What are you going to do about this problem, Julian? The guys in the Drug Squad suggested that you should attend a counsellor. What do you think?" he asked.

"Yeah, OK," I replied, hoping that this conversation would soon end.

"Well let's check out some counsellors during the week, and let's try to put all of this behind us. But in the meantime I don't want you hanging around with any of those guys, Julian," he said.

After the conversation I realised that what I was doing was leading me nowhere. I thought about the next few years. Did I want them to be the same? No. I agreed to attend a counsellor to discuss my problem. I was forbidden to contact most of my friends. At that moment I didn't care about my friends, it was time to look after number one. I didn't know just how difficult that was going to be.

I was really looking forward to celebrating my birthday in October. Four of us would celebrate our birthdays on the same day. We all went down to Murphys' early in the evening and had some joints and beers before heading into town to a club. Inside the club we had a ball. Loads of E, acid and hash. When it was over we went to a party in Ranelagh. The party was really kickin', and I met loads of friends there whom I hadn't met for ages. I met a girl called Marie-Louise, and instantly fell in love, even though I wouldn't have recognised love if it had slapped me in the face. I spent most of the evening with her, and at the end of the night a friend dropped the two of us home. It was a brilliant night from beginning to end and I was nineteen years of age!

Eventually the E weekends took their toll on my health. I had to stop working. I'd return from a weekend and sleep solidly from early Monday morning until midday on Tuesday. Marina was becoming very suspicious about my clothes. She had to wash them . . . drenched in sweat. Dad was exasperated. He was rapidly losing his patience with me. The late nights, arriving home at unearthly hours of the morning, lying about my whereabouts. He suspected I was wasting my life, and he couldn't do anything about it. Marina tried to hide her feelings about the whole thing, but, by the odd look or remark that I got from her, I knew that she knew what was going on.

"Do you fall into a river every weekend, Julian?" asked Marina.

"What do you mean?" I answered.

"Your clothes are absolutely soaked," she said.

"Well, if you danced in the clubs I'm sure your clothes would be soaked too," I said.

"I'd stop dancing if I got too sweaty. What keeps you going all night?"

"The Atmosphere. Sure I love dancing. I don't mind the sweat," I said.

"Well, *I mind* the smell when I'm washing them. It's a funny smell too, not the usual sweaty kind."

When I met my counsellor, Mary Cantwell Lynch, I found I was able to talk frankly and honestly with her. In fact she was the only person who knew the whole story about my drug involvement because she was the only one that I didn't have to lie to.

My first meeting with Mary was really strange. Dad dropped me outside her house, and said that he'd be back to collect me in about an hour. I walked up the short driveway to the porch and pressed the bell. I was so nervous. This middle-aged woman, who was very smartly dressed, opened the door.

"Mary Cantwell Lynch?"

"You must be Julian. Come in," she said, with a very pleasant look on her face.

She doesn't seem too bad, I thought, as she directed me into her front room.

"Go into the room on your right there, Julian, I'll be with you in just a moment," she said.

As I sat in a comfortable armchair I couldn't help noticing the vast number of books she had on her shelves. Books on psychology, alcoholism, drug addiction, etc.

"So how are you, Julian?" She smiled.

"Not too bad," I said.

I immediately felt stupid for saying that, as here I was seeing a counsellor.

"So tell me about yourself, Julian," she said.

I began to tell her about my parents, and then about my grandmother and her recent death, and my present situation, avoiding the mention of drugs.

"Gee, you've had it pretty bad, Julian. It hasn't been too easy, has it?" she said.

"No, not really," I replied.

Mary had a really motherly look about her. She was highly qualified, judging by the certificates on her wall. I'd say I looked like a right "case", with my bleached platinum hair, my worn-looking jacket, jeans with a big hole in the knee, and my gaunt face and black sunken eyes.

"Would you like some coffee?" she asked.

"Yes, that would be lovely, thanks," I replied.

It felt a bit strange that she hadn't asked me about drugs yet, but I knew that the question would be inevitable.

"Do you drink?" she asked.

"Yes, but very little. I'm not really mad about it," I said.

"Do you dabble in any drugs, Julian?" she asked.

Even though I was expecting the question, I still got a lump in my throat.

"Yes, I mess about with drugs," I replied.

"What type . . . hash and all that?" she asked.

"Yeah. hash, acid, Ecstasy and some speed," I said.

To my surprise, her facial expression never changed. We talked about drugs for a while and discussed my intake and my friends. After a while I heard my dad's car outside. We arranged to meet again in a fortnight and said goodbye.

On the way home in the car my dad asked what it was like.

"So how was it, Julian?" he asked.

"Not too bad . . . she was very pleasant and nice," I replied.

It was a friendly relationship. Each session lasted for about an hour, and during it I would tell her what I did that week, what I planned for the following week. Drugs were rarely mentioned at all, except for an enquiry about my intake, and gentle advice about cutting down.

"So what did you do last weekend?" said Mary.

"I went into town to a club, it wasn't too bad," I replied.

"Did you do many drugs?" she asked.

"No, not really. I think I did two E, and smoked some hash," I said.

"Was that more or less than the previous weekend?" asked Mary.

"Less. I felt quite good about it being less, and the Monday wasn't too bad either because of it," I replied.

"So you're happy about taking less?" she asked.

"Yes, it's good to reduce it now and again. Plus, it's cheaper," I said.

Eventually we got into inner feelings and

emotions. As long as I kept my appointments with Mary, my dad was happy. He thought I was dealing with my drugs problem. He never knew that I hadn't given them up, that I was still leading a sort of Jekyll and Hyde existence.

I was beginning to realise that this was a dead-end existence. I was fed up with getting high as a kite at weekends and then sleeping it off, coming down with hash, starting all over again the next weekend, and doing deals in order to pay for the habit. I was worried about the dealing. I was small time. I sold to my friends but I was already getting involved with bigger dealers. And some of the deals were messy.

"There must be a way out of this," I thought. I wasn't happy. I could see how it was affecting my parents, my relationships with normal people. The things I'd wanted to do with my life seemed to be drifting further and further away.

I'd noticed the physical and mental deterioration of both Danny and Peter. Their conversations revolved around drugs, and their speech was beginning to fall apart. They forgot arrangements for meeting places. Danny looked like a scarecrow, and Peter was becoming a deeper shade of yellow by the day. His eyes were like black holes, buried in their sockets. Poor old Harry was really losing it. Trying to carry on a conversation with him was impossible. He was beginning to forget how to string sentences together, and he couldn't focus on any subject for more than a few moments.

I was falling into a deep hole. This wasn't a comfort zone anymore, it was more like a prison. And I wanted to escape.

CHAPTER FIVE

by Gerry Madigan

I was becoming suspicious about Julian's behaviour and change of mood. Somehow I had to find out if he was involved with drugs . . . but how? I should have wondered when he decided to stop going to his swimming club. But he was still with his running club. I presumed that this was just a shift of focus.

When Julian finally moved in with us in Rathfarnham, I realised he couldn't talk to me. Not just to me. To anyone. The inventor of the Walkman should be shot for creating that most antisocial device for teenagers. He went running, played his music, went to school, and enjoyed his weekends at parties and raves. Sometimes he would come home in great form. He would be almost like the old Julian, full of chat, enthusiastic. But the next day he would turn off again. I put this down to the trauma of Heidi's death, and the move from Monaloe. All his friends lived in Cabinteely, Foxrock and Blackrock. I thought that was why he stayed away so much.

I had accepted the fact that he was now smoking regularly. I knew that he drank at weekends. Smoking was forbidden in our house because, as members of the Church of Jesus Christ of Latter-Day Saints, none of us smoked. Julian occasionally went outside for a stroll down the back garden to have his smoke. I asked him not to smoke. How could he train and run if he smoked? He always explained that he only smoked a few cigarettes a day and it didn't affect his fitness.

"You can smoke, Julian, but I think you're crazy to do it," I said.

"You'd swear I was a chain-smoker, Dad," replied Julian.

"It's irrelevant how many you smoke, Julian. The whole thing is a contradiction. Are you serious about your training and your running?" I asked.

"Of course I'm serious about it, Dad. I think you're making a mountain out of a mole-hill," he replied.

"Smoking is bad for your health, Julian, and it's disastrous for your stamina. Smoking and running are two opposite ends of the scale," I said.

"Dad, I smoke about two or three cigarettes a day. That's not going to affect my fitness level," he argued.

"It's your body, Julian, and it's your life, your career. I'm just telling you how I see it. I think you're fooling yourself," I said.

I began to question his friends. Some of the guys he brought home to stay overnight looked like drug addicts – sunken cheekbones, glazed expressions, black around the eyes, etc. After Harry was sent to St Patrick's Institution for young offenders I had a serious talk with Julian, and forbade him to associate with Harry, Danny or Peter. I was very worried about most of his friends at this stage. He told me that he wouldn't see them. He found new friends. However, they were all over in – Blackrock, Stillorgan, Foxrock. New people began phoning for Julian. These different names and voices, telephoning and leaving messages for him, made me think that he was serious about making new friends. I didn't realise that he was using them as decoys.

Weekends were a problem. He would ring me at about 11 p.m. on Friday to say that they were all invited to a party in Stillorgan or Foxrock, and would it be OK for him to stay overnight with Gordon? I'd checked with the parents of these guys in the past, so I presumed it *would* be all right. Sometimes I'd ring them on the night just to make sure that his story was true. Sometimes there would be confusion about the exact house, or parent, or name. The stories began to get very complicated. I thought all of them must have been collaborating with one another to make up these stories to throw us off the scent (I was right!).

I could never understand why he needed a rucksack with T-shirts, shorts and all sorts of things . . . going to a dance! But I was even more mystified when he arrived home on a Sunday night with his shorts, T-shirts, sweaters drenched in sweat. This wasn't normal sweat. It was as if he had left his clothes lying in a bath of water overnight. The smell was disturbing.

"How come your clothes are in such a state after the weekend, Julian?" I asked.

"It gets very hot at the raves, Dad," he replied.

"But your clothes are absolutely drenched," I said.

"I know . . . sure I dance all night, Dad." He smiled.

"Have none of the other parents asked about their sons' clothes?" I asked.

"Yeah, of course they have. But you sweat when you're dancing so much," he said.

"Are you sure you're not taking any of this E stuff to make you dance so long?" I asked.

"For goodness sake, Dad. What do you take me for? I'm young and fit. It's no problem to dance all night at the weekends. I'm sure you went out dancing at weekends when you were my age," he said with an innocent look on his face.

"I never sweated like that, Julian, and I never stayed out for three nights in a row," I replied.

The explanations were convincing, but I didn't believe them. Something wasn't right. It was time to start serious investigations. I'd already got him into embarrassing situations by ringing parents' homes late at night to check where he was. I didn't want to destroy his credibility with his friends. But I had to put the pieces of this jigsaw puzzle together. I decided to make some calls. First on the list was his running coach.

"Hello, Larry, this is Gerry Madigan here, Julian Madigan's father," I said.

"Ah, Julian's dad. How's Julian?" he asked.

"Oh, he's fine. I was just ringing you to ask how his training is coming along?" I asked.

"Well, I don't know. That's why I asked you how he was keeping. I haven't seen Julian for about six months," he said.

"Are you serious?" I asked.

"Absolutely. In fact I was wondering what

happened to him. He has tremendous potential, but he started missing training sessions some time ago. I had a chat with him about it, and suggested he make up his mind if he's serious about running or not," said Larry.

"Well this is news to me. As far I'm concerned, Julian has been training two nights a week at least for the past year," I said.

"Well he hasn't been training with me," he replied.

"I appreciate this information, Larry, and I'll have to talk to Julian this evening about this."

"Not at all. You're very welcome. Give him my regards," Larry said.

That was the first shock. I put down the phone. Why had Julian deceived me for the past six months? What was he doing if he wasn't training? Why would he say he was training if he wasn't? I couldn't wait for him to come home.

My adrenalin was pumping. Something was going on . . . I knew it. But which parent would I ask? Harry's, Danny's or Peter's? Maybe they know nothing about this either. But I had to talk to someone. I couldn't rely on Julian. There must be more to his story than forgetfulness. This was organised and pre-arranged deception. I decided to ring Peter Burton's parents.

"Hello, could I speak with Mrs Burton?" I asked.

"Yes, Mary Burton speaking,"

"I'm Gerry Madigan, Julian Madigan's father," I said.

"Ah yes, I know Julian well. He's a lovely lad," she said.

"Thank you very much. But I'm just a little concerned about a few things, Mrs Burton, and I don't know whether you can help me or not," I said.

"About Julian?" she asked.

"Well, it's about the whole gang that he hangs around with. I know they go to a lot of these raves together. But I'm a bit concerned about these long stayovers. The sweaty clothes after the raves. I can't quite put my finger on it, but something's not quite right," I said.

"Do you not know what's going on?" she asked.

"I don't. That's why I'm ringing you. Do you know something that I don't?" I asked.

"They're all on drugs," she said.

"What?" I replied in astonishment.

"Yes, they're all taking hash, acid and Ecstasy," she insisted.

"Are you sure?" I asked.

"Of course I'm sure. We've had Peter in Coolmine Drugs Centre on two occasions in the past few months. Our lives have been almost destroyed because of Peter's involvement with drugs. We can't leave any money, cheque books, credit cards lying around the house anymore. My husband is worried sick over the whole thing," she said.

"My goodness, I'm absolutely shocked. And is Julian involved too?" I asked.

"I don't know how deeply Julian is involved, but I know for certain that Peter, Danny and Harry are very deeply involved," she said.

"This is dreadful. I'll have to do something about this urgently," I said.

"Well, I'm delighted that you're willing to accept the facts. I've already spoken with Danny's mother, but she doesn't accept a word of it. She's positive that her Danny has nothing to do with drugs, but I know for a fact that they're all taking drugs," she said.

"Thank you for telling me all of this, and I'm sorry to hear about Peter," I said.

"Well, good luck with whatever you decide to do and, if I can be of any help, don't be afraid to call me," she said.

As I replaced the receiver my hands were trembling. How could this be happening. Julian on drugs! In my years in the recording industry I had seen so many people get heavily involved in drugs.

So many lives destroyed. Did Julian have any idea what he was getting himself into. This was serious. But what now? How could I handle this the right way? Where could I get help . . . professional help?

My mind was racked with all sorts of guilt feelings. This must have something to do with our separation. Perhaps it was because of my marriage to Marina. It was the move from Monaloe to Rathfarnham . . . maybe Heidi's death sparked it off. But I didn't even know for absolute certain if he was definitely involved. Or did I? Yes I did. The writing was on the wall, this was no time for denial. This called for action, not conjecture. Reasons didn't matter. Julian was abusing drugs, I had to help him stop . . . somehow.

I'd worried about Julian's friends, and I'd been right. I had to find out more about where he was going, who he was with. Where did they get the drugs, what were they taking, how and where did they take them?

"Julian, that's someone for you," I called, as I pressed the "record" button on the answering machine. "You can take it in the hall." I closed my office door. When I played back the recorded conversation I nearly passed out with shock.

"Hello," said Julian.

"Hello, Madzer? Danny, here. I told your old man I was somebody else. Can you talk?" he said.

"Yeah, sure. What's happening, man?" said Julian.

"Where did you go last Friday when you left me and Harry?" he asked.

"I just went down to Jacko's for a while. Where did you go?" asked Julian.

"Remember that stuff we picked up from Peter's mate?" he asked.

"Yeah," replied Julian.

"Well, we went down to the Creole Café and had some of it. What a whack off it, man. We were flying for hours after it. Wait'll you have some of it . . . talk about strong stuff," he said.

"I can't wait," said Julian.

"Do you have any E for tonight?" asked Danny.

"No, but Harry and I are picking up some in Baggot Street before we meet yourself and Peter at the club," said Julian.

"Good, because I gave Harry fifty quid to get some for me. How many did you do last weekend, Madzer?" he asked.

"Two on Friday, two on Saturday, and just one on Sunday," Julian replied.

"Myself and Peter did three each on Sunday night . . . we were bombed out of our heads," he said.

"Well, listen I'll see you at the club at about eight o'clock tonight, OK?" asked Julian.

"OK. See you then, Madzer," he said.

So Julian was still meeting Harry, Danny and Peter all this time. Before Julian went out that night, I decided to ask him who had telephoned him. I'd known it was Danny when I answered the phone, but I wanted to see if he would tell me the truth.

"That was Eoin's friend, John. We met him last weekend. He was just making arrangements to meet us all tonight again," replied Julian.

"I hope you're not meeting Danny, Peter or Harry tonight, Julian," I said.

"No, I'm meeting that guy, John, and Eoin and Gordon and that gang," he replied.

This was treacherous territory. I would have to tread very carefully from now on. I couldn't let Julian know that I'd recorded his telephone conversation, and yet I had to do something with the knowledge that I'd gained. How was I going to stop this?

During the next few weeks I tried to record every phone call that Julian received. It was difficult to record calls when he phoned out, but I got enough information over those few weeks to let me know that Julian and his so-called friends at this point in his life were taking drugs. I didn't know what Strawberries, Doves, Mad Bastards or Microdots were then, but I had a good idea that they weren't talking about computer components.

Now that I had some facts, I had to do something with them. I had to devise a clever plan to help Julian break away from this scene. I talked with a friend of mine, Liam Gallagher, who suggested that I contact the Juvenile Liaison Officer in my local Garda Station. This sounded a little bit drastic at the time, but he explained that the Juvenile Liaison Officer might be able to throw some light on the subject, and maybe give me some idea of what to do.

Could Julian be *dealing* in drugs? Hardly likely but, up until a few weeks before, I couldn't have imagined him even *taking* drugs. Would they try to arrest him? Would they have his interest at heart, or would they be career-driven individuals looking for a conviction? I'd already read too many stories about young people dying from Ecstasy. I didn't want my son to die in some club. I'd had enough sleepless nights and anxious weekends. I had to make a decision and accept the consequences.

"I'm Liam Nicholson, the JLO attached to Rathfarnham.

How can I help you?" asked this pleasant looking gentleman in plain clothes.

"My name is Gerry Madigan, and I think my son is involved in drugs." I sat down at the table in a very drab looking interview room at the Garda station.

"Do you know if he's definitely involved?" he asked.

"Yes, he's definitely taking Ecstasy," I said.

"Is he involved in dealing drugs?" he asked.

"Gosh, I hope not," I replied.

"Has he taken heroin or cocaine?" he asked.

"I hope not, but I really haven't a clue how far into it he's gone," I replied.

"Well, the main thing you want to do is stop him, I suppose?" he said.

"Of course. But I don't know anything about the drug scene. That's why I'm here. I don't even know if you can help me," I said.

"I'll give you any support that I can," he said.

"What's the first step? Where do I go from here?" I asked.

"Let me get some general information from you first, and then give me a few days to come up with a plan of action. What's your son's name?" he asked.

That was my first step in trying to help Julian break

out of the drug culture. Liam Nicholson gave me a crash course on drugs awareness. He gave me clues about Julian's behaviour. He told me to watch for mood swings, any sudden violent outbursts, dilated eyes, not eating regularly, disruptive sleep and any sort of incoherence.

My next contact with Liam was when the Drug Squad arrived at my door to search Julian's room. What a relief to see Liam's face behind the Drug Squad detectives.

Marina and I had a long conversation with Liam that night, while the two detectives were upstairs interrogating Julian.

"Look, I know how upsetting this is for you both, but by bringing Julian face to face with the reality of what he's involved with, it may help him to think about stopping," said Liam.

"My goodness, Liam, I felt so sorry for poor Julian when they marched him upstairs," said Marina.

"I know, but imagine how sorry you'd feel for him if they were marching him off to jail." Liam said.

"This whole drugs thing must be absolutely rampant, Liam," I said.

"You've no idea how bad it is. But if we could only get the parents to recognise their children's behaviour, and then cooperate with us in trying to steer them away from the drug culture, we'd have a better chance of tackling the problem," he said.

"Yes, but it's the initial shock of realising that your son's involved with drugs that almost paralyses you. I've been going around feeling absolutely numb since I discovered what's been happening," I said.

"Well there is help available. We're here to help you in any way that we can, and I would recommend that Julian starts seeing a counsellor immediately. Now that at least part of the problem is out in the open, perhaps you can convince him to attend a good counsellor."

When the Drug Squad detectives came downstairs they explained that they suspected that he was taking hash, and possibly acid and E, but that they felt we'd caught him in time. They'd warned him and counselled him about the dangers of drug abuse. The most important thing to come from that night was the advice that Julian should immediately start seeing a counsellor.

I found a counsellor who specialised in dealing with young people with drug abuse problems. Julian agreed to meet her. I didn't know whether this was going to work, but at least it was step in the right direction. We were now on level ground. Julian admitted that he had taken hash and a little bit of acid and E, but he said he wasn't an addict and he didn't have a major problem with drugs.

"Dad, you used to take a drink. Well taking a little bit of hash is exactly the same thing, except you don't have the hangover the next day," reasoned Julian.

"And what about the acid and the Ecstasy? I suppose they're harmless too?" I asked.

"I'm not an addict, Dad. I've taken one or two at a party for a bit of a laugh. I don't know what all the fuss is about, I don't have a drug problem," he said.

"That's what chronic alcoholics keep saying to themselves, Julian, and eventually they convince themselves that they don't have a problem. But they *do*, Julian," I said.

"Look, Dad, I said I'd attend a counsellor to discuss the hash. I won't be touching any more of the other stuff . . . as I said, it was only a once-off bit of fun," he said.

Should I be so naïve as to give him the benefit of the doubt, or should I carry on with my own plan of action and follow this through to the very end? He had a problem all right, but he had to be brought to his senses.

The rules were drastically changed. No more raves. No more contact with any of his previous friends, who I knew were on drugs. No more stayovers without specific arrangements being made with the parents. Everything seemed to be falling into place, and I hoped that we had nipped the problem in the bud. But I went on recording Julian's phone calls.

I was sure he wasn't seeing the old gang now. He kept on saying no to his friends when they phoned and suggested meeting and buying Ecstasy. But one day he put down the phone after a conversation, grabbed his bag, and headed out the door. I rushed into my office and played back the telephone conversation.

"Hiya, Madzer. It's me, Danny. Can you talk?" he said.

"Yeah, sure. It's cool," replied Julian.

"Look, I've got a hundred quid with me, and Peter's given me fifty quid. Could you come up with fifty quid, because we can get two hundred quid's worth of E at a bargain deal?" he asked.

"I doubt it, but I could try," said Julian.

"We need to pick it up from Jacko's at two o'clock this afternoon but I've got to be at work then. Could you meet me with your money, and I'll give you the rest of it, then you pick it up from Jacko?" he asked.

"OK. Meet at the usual place?" Julian said.

"Yeah, at the entrance to the St Stephen's Green

Centre. But you'll have to get into town in the next half an hour," he said.

I'd heard enough. I charged out the door, got into my car, and headed straight into town. I parked in the Setanta Centre, and made my way up to the St Stephen's Green Centre. I'd no idea what I was going to do, but I was going to do something. Feeling like a sleuth from an Agatha Christie novel, I stood at a magazine rack in the shop on the corner opposite the St Stephen's Green Centre. With a magazine in my hand, I had a clear view of the Centre. Within minutes I saw Danny arrive and stand at the corner. It seemed like ages, but about five minutes later I saw Julian arrive. He showed Danny something. I stood on tiptoe to have a better look, I saw that it was my antique sword cane. What on *earth* was he doing with my antique sword cane?

The two of them crossed the road towards the shop where I was hiding! I buried myself among the customers and magazine racks as they passed the door and headed down Grafton Street. I followed them from a safe distance. Their first port of call was an antique dealer/pawnshop in Temple Bar. I watched them go in. They came out about three minutes later. They still had the sword cane. At this stage I realised they were trying to sell the sword cane. They called into about four more antique dealers in Clarendon Street and the Powerscourt Townhouse Centre, but obviously none of them were interested in buying a sword cane. I was following them at a reasonable distance when they came out of the Powerscourt Townhouse Centre, but suddenly they turned and headed back . . . straight for me. I turned on my heel, down a flight of stairs, into a travel shop and buried my head in a travel brochure. About three minutes later I went back on the trail, but they'd vanished. I spent about twenty minutes searching for them in the Grafton Street area. Eventually I noticed Julian's bicycle locked to the railings of Stephen's Green. I remembered the telephone conversation. I decided to wait here until they returned from their visit to Baggot Street.

Julian eventually arrived back to his bicycle on his own. As he unlocked the bicycle and strapped the sword cane to the crossbar, I approached him.

"Well, Julian, what are you doing with my sword cane?" I asked.

"Hi, Dad. I was just trying to see if it was worth any money. I thought you might need the cash," he said, as if it was the most natural thing in the world.

"Julian, I was in Duke Street, and I saw you and Danny walking down Grafton Street with the sword cane, so I followed you. You were trying to sell it. And I thought you weren't seeing Danny anymore either?"

"I just met him at the top of Grafton Street, and he said he'd come with me," said Julian.

"Let's go home, Julian," I said. This guy deserved an Oscar.

I was getting nowhere. How could he possibly expect me to believe all this nonsense? He was an expert at deception by now. It was time that I became an expert at detection too. I wondered if he was still taking the stuff, or was the counselling having any affect at all. I couldn't let him know that I knew about his pre-arranged meeting. That would have blown my only source of direct information – taping the phone calls. The ice was getting thinner. I had to tread even more carefully. The problem wasn't over yet . . . not by a long shot.

CHAPTER SIX

BREAKING OUT

In the autumn of 1994 I was becoming disillusioned with the drugs scene. After the visit from the Drug Squad I wanted to get out of the whole mess. In my more rational moments, I realised that I'd been doing the same thing every weekend for the past four years. Even when I was taking drugs I knew that. It began to bother me. My weekends were getting longer and longer. The intake of drugs was becoming more varied and larger in quantity. I could see that I was really being sucked into this culture, but there weren't many exit doors visible.

I always had to be careful about where I said I was sleeping over because my dad had this annoying habit of checking up on me by telephoning the homes of my friends. I'd become a master of deception. As I've said before, my friends and I were usually able to concoct a believable story as to our whereabouts. The excuses varied from twenty-first birthday parties, welcome-home parties, leaving-the-job parties, going-away parties to broken bicycles, missed buses, no taxis, no money, etc. I rationalised my conduct in a weird way. I'd decide to stay out all night because it wasn't worth going home at 4.00 a.m. in case I woke them up at home, so I'd wait until 10.00 a.m. . . . Very considerate of me!

My dad had forbidden me to see certain "undesirable" friends. This meant using false names on the telephone, false addresses for the parties, etc. "Julian, I don't want you hanging around with Danny Fox and Peter Burton," said Dad.

"OK. But why?" I asked.

"You know why, Julian. We've talked about this so many times. Do you not realise that they're going nowhere, and they're taking you with them. They're both on drugs, and you said you're giving all of that up now, so they're no good for you. They're wasters, Julian," he said.

"Yeah, I suppose you're right," I said, just to keep the peace.

"You know I'm right, Julian. I'm only looking out for you," he said.

"Yeah, I understand."

THE INCIDENT

In December 1994 something happened. "The Incident" stretched over a four-week period, from the end of November to the end of December. I'd started hanging around with two of my old acquaintances again, doing small deals. Yes, two of the guys whom my dad had told me to keep away from. I don't know what it was about those two jerks but they were really bad luck.

I was selling a few Es for Alan, a friend of mine, because I needed the money. My habit still cost me a lot of money, even though I'd cut down. I slept in one Saturday evening and because of that I lost a weekend of selling. I was in a mess. I couldn't just hand back part-money and part-drugs. That just wasn't done. There was a strict code of business practice in this scene. It was too awkward for your supplier. It had to be all money. I'd told Alan that I could sell these Es – he wouldn't have to worry about the money. The next day was Sunday. I called down to Murphys'. I knew that they'd all be there recovering from Saturday night. I knocked on the door. Dots opened it. I went into the front room. They were all there with their heads hanging to bits, their eyes dead and sunken back into their heads. I asked to speak to Alan on his own, outside the house.

I knew that the excuse of "sleeping in" wouldn't be good enough for Alan, so I decided to change it in the hope of getting some sympathy instead of aggro.

"What's up, Madzer?" he said in a happy voice as he came outside. He was tripped off his head.

"Look, there's a small problem with the Es," I said.

You could say that his facial expression changed.

"My dad found them on me last night, and that's why I couldn't go out with you all," I lied.

"Do you still have them?" he said anxiously.

"Yes, I have them. I gave my dad a really good cock and bull story and he gave them back to me, but I might have to go for tests," I said, lying through my teeth.

"Don't worry about it, Madzer. Would you be able to sell them by next Friday?" he asked.

All I could think of was, yes, it worked, I'd got an extra week to sell this stuff.

"Yeah, I'm sure I could," I replied.

"Fine, then that's all right. Do you want a smoke?" he asked.

"Yeah, sure," I said.

We went back inside and joined the rest of the gang.

The following Thursday I met Danny Fox. We decided to go out to a club as Danny had just got a fresh batch of E and was eager to sell them in order to buy some more for Saturday. I just *had* to sell mine to get the money to give to Alan the next day. Foxey owed me an E from a while ago, and he repaid me that night. We were both buzzing around town that night, off our heads, having a good laugh and catching up with old times.

We called into one of our regular haunts to see if we could shift some Es. We met a few mates and had a pint, but the place was empty. Not much chance of selling any E in here we thought. After a while one of Danny's mates said that we should go to The Friary. It was supposed to be brilliant up there on Thursday nights. I asked one of the other guys what it was like and he said it was great, but that it might be difficult for me to get in. We went up to The Friary with Danny's friend. It was only a few hundred metres away from where we were. On the way we stalled to hide our merchandise somewhere safe on ourselves. Down our jocks. Difficult to search, and rarely found.

We were met by five bouncers, one who looked more like a punter than a bouncer. They were all well over six foot in height, and the punter-looking one had a diamond-shaped object hanging out of his cheek. Not the type of person you'd like to meet on a dark night. The rest of the bouncers looked sound enough. I shared a joke with one of them, which helped settle my nerves a bit as we walked down a tunnel to the cashier. As we entered, our first impression was that this was a kickin' place. "I'd say we'll sell some stuff here all right," I thought.

We put our jackets in the cloakroom and wandered around the club. I went up to the bar to get a drink. Danny noticed a group of attractive girls, and we started dancing close to them. Suddenly I realised that I wasn't here to enjoy myself. I was here to sell E. I asked some people if they wanted any. I needed to sell a minimum of twelve in order to be able to give Alan £160 the next day. It didn't go too well. I sold six. I was beginning to get frantic.

Danny took me aside. "Don't worry about it Madzer, Alan's not going to kill you. You still have enough Es to make up the price, don't you?" he said.

"Yeah, I suppose," I replied.

After about twenty minutes dancing and talking we decided to leave the club and call up to Jacko's flat in Baggot Street. Jacko was a friend and Danny's supplier. He used to be my supplier too, but we'd had that "bloody nose" argument over money. In fact it was over me being late with his money, and he'd freaked about it. He made such a song and dance about it that I thought it best to change supplier. It was about 1.30 a.m. as we walked up Baggot Street.

Danny assured me that Jacko would be awake and that it was OK to call up at this time. "Maybe you can get about thirty Es off him on credit yourself, Madzer," said Foxey.

"Yeah, that wouldn't be bad at all," I said.

Jacko lived in a lovely one-bedroom apartment. He was a *real* drug dealer. That was his full-time occupation. He did it for a living, and a very good living too. He was a professional. Danny, Harry, Peter and myself were amateurs who dabbled in small deals among our friends. Jacko was in a different league altogether. He'd been dealing for quite a short while but, in that short while, he'd got in with the right people (or wrong people). He was twenty-four years-old and had a kid who lived with his mother, Jacko's ex-girlfriend. We pressed the buzzer at the entrance to the courtyard, opened the door and walked in towards the entrance of his flat. There was a black steel gate at the entrance.

Jacko came down the stairs and switched on the light. "All right lads . . . what's the story?" he said with a surprised look on his face.

"Ah not too bad . . . yourself?" I replied.

He opened the gate and we went up the open stairs. "To your right, Madzer," he said.

I opened the door and walked inside. The apartment was cosy. Expensively furnished with comfortable chairs and all mod cons. We sat around the coffee table in the centre of the main lounge area. The subdued side-lighting gave it a luxurious feel.

"How are things, Madzer? Long time no see," he said.

"Not too bad. Just messing about. When did you move into this pad, Jacko?" I asked.

"About a month ago. So where were you guys tonight?" he said.

"We went up to our regular local but it was pretty crap, so we went over to check out a new dance place called The Friary," I answered.

"It was good and packed," added Danny.

"Yeah, I heard that it was a good place, but I haven't been there yet myself," Jacko said.

"Jacko, would you be able to fix us up with about

thirty Es tonight . . . that is if you have them?" asked Danny.

"Yeah, no worries." He went in search of his bag of tricks. He returned a few minutes later with a bag full of E.

"Could you sort me out with about twenty of those E, Jacko?" I asked.

"Just wait until I check how many I have." He counted.

"Yeah, I can sort you out with twenty. But lads, I'll need the money for these by tea-time on Saturday. All right?" he said firmly.

"Yeah, that's fine," we answered. He handed us our stuff. We talked for a little while longer and then we left his apartment.

The minute we got outside we realised that we'd missed the last bus home. We decided to take another E and go down to Mr Burger in Grafton Street. We took the Es out of the bag and realised that we had no water to wash them down with. But our need and greed for these little white pills made it easy for us to take them without water, even though the taste was absolutely disgusting. It was worth it for the buzz, so we necked them . . . our third E each that night.

We arrived at Mr Burger. I grabbed a seat by the

window while Danny went up to get two teas. As we drank the tea we began to come up on our E. This is almost the most exciting part of taking E, the anticipation. We put about four pounds into the juke-box and played our favourite music. The rest of the night was spent in Mr Burger, drinking tea and smoking hash.

We took our fourth E at about 6.30 a.m., and eventually left Mr Burger at 9.30 in the morning! Our first port of call was the St Stephen's Green Centre to get some breakfast, even though we were still flying on the effects of the last E, and we weren't really hungry. It seemed to be the thing to do at that hour of the morning in downtown Dublin.

We went down to the Regent Barber Shop to get our hair cut before we headed back out to Cabinteely. On the way home we called in to see if Peter Burton was at work, but he was away again. He never kept a job for more than a few weeks. We knew he must be at home, so we decided we'd call for him on our way into town later that day. Danny and I walked back to his house in Cabinteely. We were absolutely exhausted by the time we got there. Danny told me to tell his mother that he had stayed at my house the previous night if she asked any questions. Sure enough she did ask, and I told her the lie.

In Danny's bedroom we decided to change our gear, put some stuff into a bag, and then get out of the house before his father came home. We went up to the compound in Cabinteely forest to crash out . . . it was now 4.30 in the afternoon, and we hadn't been in bed since Wednesday night. The compound was a large area of ground up in the middle of Cabinteely forest where the County Council left tractors and trailers. Under a corrugated roof we found a large sheet of plywood which we lay on. The idea of smoking a nice relaxing spliff was very appealing. We rolled a couple of joints. We lay there enjoying the smoke, making plans for that night, and fell asleep . . . exhausted.

It was pitch dark when we woke up, and we were frozen. We put on our shoes and jackets, and called down to Peter Burton. We asked him if he'd come into town with us.

"Ah no, lads. I'm totally knackered," Peter said.

"Aren't you selling any Es tonight?" asked Danny.

"No, I'm not pushed. I'll sell them tomorrow night," he answered.

"Sound enough then," I said.

We told him about our exploits of the previous night. The look on his face was something else.

When Danny and I arrived in town, we headed for the local club. But, to our surprise, we weren't allowed in. We tried a few other clubs, but we weren't going to be let in anywhere tonight. We went back to our local club, where a friend of ours had got a gig doing DJ. After a short while, a few friends of mine came along and we chatted for a while outside the club. Because Danny and I couldn't get into the gig, we decided to go back to Mr Burger to wait until it was finished. Then we'd find a party to go to. At about 2.30 a.m. we headed back to our local, just as everyone was leaving. We chatted with a group of our friends. Danny said he would go on up to Jacko's flat, and that I should follow him.

As I hung around outside the club, an old acquaintance of mine, Frank Ryan, came out. He had just returned from Africa. He asked me if I had any Es to sell.

"How many do you want?" I asked.

"Just two," he said.

As I took them out of my pocket, he reached for the bag of E.

"What are you playing at, Frank?" I said.

"Give them to me . . . they're my Es," he said.

"Quit the messing, and give them back," I said, trying to get his hands off the bag.

Frank seized them and went off with a group of his friends. It sounds really straightforward, but remember that I hadn't slept for forty-eight hours, and I'd been doing drugs during all that time. I was so disoriented that I didn't realise what was happening . . . everything seemed to happen in slow motion. My mental and physical state left me in no position to retaliate. He'd just taken about fifty E from me. That was the last I saw of Frank Ryan and my bag of Es.

I realised that I was deeply in debt and I would have to fix that. I followed Danny back to Jacko's flat, and explained to Jacko what had happened.

"Look, Jacko, there's a bit of a problem with those Es," I said.

"What do you mean, Madzer?" he asked.

"They're not in my hands anymore, I've just been ripped off. But don't worry, I'll have the money for you, I have some cash in reserve," I said.

"What happened, Madzer? Who ripped you off?" asked Danny.

"It was Frank Ryan," I replied.

"That guy's a bloody lunatic," said Danny.

"Look, Madzer, I'll give you a couple of days to sort it out," Jacko said.

"Thanks. Cheers, Jacko," I said.

Danny and I left and got a taxi at Jury's Hotel and

headed back to Deansgrange. Danny went home. I went into Murphys', because Dots Murphy was having a going-away party. The party was kicking. Everybody was off their heads. I mentioned the incident to Robin Murphy and Bobby Doyle, and they said that they would try and help me out.

"What's up, Madzer? You don't look the best, man," Robin said.

"I've just had a bag of E ripped off," I said.

"How did that happen?" asked Bobby.

"I was waiting outside the club in town. Frank Ryan came out and just grabbed them off me," I said.

"Why did you let him away with it, Madzer? Why didn't you grab them back?" asked Robin.

"I don't know. I was absolutely stoned. I haven't been to bed for the past two days. Everything happened so fast, and yet it was like slow motion." I explained.

"So what are you going to do?" asked Bobby.

"I don't know yet. I'll have to think of some plan. I still owe Jacko for the bag of E. I'll have to get the money somewhere . . . somehow," I said.

"Look, we'll help you out some way, Madzer. Won't we, Robin?" said Bobby.

"Yeah, sure. We'll help you sort something out, Madzer," agreed Robin.

I took two E. I was well on my way. Whacker and Moloney did the music. The night was really good.

In the morning, Bobby called me aside and handed me a large bag of E. "Madzer, do you want to sell these for me?" he asked.

"How much are they?" I asked.

"Ten pounds fifty each," he said.

"Yeah, I'll take them off you. When do I have to have the money for you?" I asked. "Tuesday night," Bobby replied.

I took the bag of E and thought about it. If I sold all the E, I'd have enough money to pay back what I'd lost that night. There was a big gig in town the following night. I could sell the E there.

As I walked through town, I asked various friends of mine if they wanted to buy E. Most of them said yes. I got to the gig, it was jam-packed. The queue outside was about fifty metres long. As I walked along the queue, I noticed faces of friends. I jumped into the queue with a few of them. Slowly but surely we edged our way to the front door. We made our way inside. The noise inside was deafening.

Suddenly a voice sounded in my ear, "Do you have any of my money, Madzer?" I turned around and saw that it was Alan.

"Yeah, just give us a minute, Alan," I replied.

He was quite surprised to see me pull out the money from my pocket and pay him what I owed him. "To be honest, Madzer, I didn't think you'd come up with it tonight," he said.

"Ah well, surprises do happen," I said.

I left Alan, and went about my business of trying to get rid of this bag of E. I met up with Danny, and told him the story of Bobby giving me the bag of E. He said that was sound, and that it should help the situation. We found a nice place by the emergency exit where we could dance and ask passers-by if they wanted any E. There were bouncers here but they were OK. They asked for a few tokes of our joints, and chatted to us. The night was good, but I didn't sell enough Es. Afterwards, myself and a few of the gang from Deansgrange ended up at a party in Ballinteer. I don't remember much of it, because I hadn't got any sleep since midday on Thursday afternoon, and this was Sunday morning. I looked and felt like a zombie.

I fell asleep about an hour after arriving, and when I woke up I was in a bit of a panic because all the lads from Deansgrange had left. I didn't know anybody else at the party. I left shortly afterwards, and got a taxi home.

I woke up on Monday morning, and got the usual

lecture from Dad . . . where had I been, with whom, etc. I gave the usual answers . . . the going-away party, no phone near, missing the bus, etc. I knew by the look on his face, that these excuses were wearing thin. I spent the next week wondering what I was going to do about Bobby and these Es. The following day I went into town and tried to pawn my Omega watch, but the pawnbroker only offered sixty pounds so I had to think of something else. Jacko's flat was close enough to the pawnbrokers so I decided to call into him.

"How are things, Jacko?" I asked.

"Not too bad, struggling along as usual," he said sarcastically.

"Remember that little incident last weekend?" I asked.

"Yes," he said.

"Well, here are the eighteen E which I owe you," I said, handing him the remainder of Bobby's bag of E.

"So are we clear now?" I asked.

"Yeah, that's fine," he said.

"Would you be interested in taking an ounce of speed off me, Madzer?" he asked.

"What would you be charging me?" I asked.

"A hundred and fifty pounds. That's cheap, because it's a good ounce," he said.

I worked out quickly in my head what type of profit I could make from selling an ounce of speed. "Yeah, no problem. When will I have to pay for it?"

"No rush. In around two weeks or so," he said.

Nice one, I thought. I'd be able to make about £250 on this, give it to Bobby, and explain that I'd have the balance in about a week. Now, I think I must have been absolutely mad. When I left Jacko's flat, I didn't know, and neither did he, that it would be the last time that I would see Jacko.

The following week I snorted and sold speed. It is different from acid and Ecstasy, even though Ecstasy is made mainly from amphetamine, which is the chemical name for speed. Speed is a class "B" drug which means it is a lesser offence to get caught with speed than it is to get caught with Ecstasy. Speed is like a massive shot of adrenalin. It literally speeds up the metabolic rate and makes you feel really hyper. When you're on speed you're like a hen on a hot griddle, you can't stay still for a moment, it's all go go go. The problem with taking speed is that you end up with raw nostrils. In order to get the best hit out of speed, you need to snort it up your nose. To counteract the discomfort of the burning sensation in your nostrils, you need to snort cold water . . . messy business.

I made enough money to pay for it, but I never got around to calling in to see Jacko. Bobby had been ringing the house at least once a day at this stage and many of his mates, who were also my friends, were also ringing the house. It was almost two weeks since Bobby had given me the bag of Es and I knew that he would be frantic about the situation. Harry rang me on the Thursday night. I arranged to meet him in town at 8.30 outside the National Art Gallery. My father was extremely suspicious about my conduct during that week, and in fact I was restricted to the vicinity of Rathfarnham.

"Julian, you're falling back into this ridiculous routine of staying overnight with various friends again. Look at the state of yourself. You're absolutely exhausted. Do you realise how long you slept after the weekend?" said Dad.

"I was just tired, Dad. We stayed up a bit late on the Saturday night at Dots Murphy's going-away party. I'm sorry," I said.

"That's not good enough, Julian. We've talked and talked about this over and over again. You rang me on Thursday to say that you'd be staying in Bobby's house because you missed the last bus home. Then you rang on Friday to ask if you could go to that gig in town that your friends were doing DJ at. But you never came home, and I get a phone call on Saturday asking if you could stay in Murphys' for Dots Murphy's going-away party. Now cop on, Julian, do you think I came down in the last shower?" he asked.

"I'm sorry, Dad. It won't happen again," I said.

"You bet your life it won't happen again because, as and from now, you're grounded," he said.

"What do you mean grounded?" I asked.

"I mean you're not going outside this area in future. I want to know where you are at all times, and I'm not going to spend my time ringing Bobby and Robin and everybody else trying to find out where you are," he said.

"OK, I'll stay in the Rathfarnham area," I said.

I left the house and said that I was just calling up to a neighbour's house for a while, and that I'd be back at about 10.30 p.m.

I caught the bus into town, and brought some money for Jacko, and some speed in case I might sell some. Harry and I met as arranged and went up to a local pub to discuss the problem that I was having with Bobby.

"You're up shit creek without a paddle, Madzer, concerning this Bobby thing," said Harry.

"What do you mean 'up shit creek'? I'm doing the best I can to fix the problem," I said.

"Well, Bobby's really worried that he's not going to get his money for that bag of E he gave you. You haven't rung him or anything, and he doesn't know what's happening. He said he keeps ringing your house but you're never in," said Harry.

"Harry, I told you what happened with the stuff. I got some E from Jacko, and some from Alan, but Frank Ryan stole them from me. So I owed them the money for that E, but I'd no E to sell in order to get the money to give them. Do you understand?" I asked.

"Yeah, but what about Bobby's bag of E and Bobby's money? It's not fair on him, Madzer. He has to get paid for that E," said Harry.

"I know, Harry, and I'm going to pay him, but it's just going to take a lot longer than I thought. Look, I've already sold the bag of E that Bobby gave me, but I had to pay Jacko and Alan because they were pressurising me for money," I said.

"So how are you going to pay Bobby?" he said.

"Look, Harry, I'm in a real fix here. I'm caught right in the middle, but I'm trying to sort it out. I just need a little bit more time to organise things," I said.

"Well I think you should let Bobby know, Madzer. He was also under massive pressure from his supplier and he had to give his record decks as security for a loan of the money to pay him," said Harry.

"And who's supplying Bobby?" I asked.

"I don't know, but he's obviously somebody you don't mess around with. Bobby wouldn't have sold his decks if he wasn't under pressure," said Harry.

We ended up having a few too many pints laced with speed. We played pool upstairs for a couple of hours. By this stage it was near midnight. I suggested that we try some of the clubs in town and Harry agreed. I didn't care about the time. I was late anyway.

As we arrived at the main entrance to St Stephen's Green, I saw Billy Stockton and his bimbo girlfriend. It was difficult *not* to notice him. He stood about six foot four inches tall, a body-builder, massive physique, closely shaven hair. He walked like a cowboy gunslinger and had a voice to match. Not the sort of person you'd want to mess with. He worked as a bouncer in some of the roughest night-clubs in the city. Some of the stories about Stockton's fighting exploits were horrific . . . smashed faces, broken jaws. His victims always ended up in hospital. I didn't know that he was Bobby's dealer/supplier. But I *did* know that he was friendly with Bobby.

Harry and I turned to head in the other direction. Suddenly, as if from nowhere, I felt as if I'd been hit with a sledge-hammer . . . *smack!* It floored me. I looked up from where I lay on the ground. Stockton towered over me.

"You better have that money for Bobby, Madzer," he roared.

"What are you doing, Stockton?" screamed Harry.

"Stay out of this, Harry. It's none of your business," boomed Stockton.

"Yeah, stay out of it," squeaked his blonde girlfriend.

"You better have that money, Madzer. I'm warning you. If you don't pay Bobby that £400 by next week, you'll end up in hospital," shouted Stockton.

"Yeah, I'll get it," I said.

I couldn't believe what was happening. This was a very public place, plenty of people passing by, and not one person came to my help. As quickly as it started, it ended. Stockton and his girlfriend made off rapidly, leaving me dazed, and Harry bewildered. Harry helped me to my feet. My head was spinning and my face was partly numb, partly on fire. I guess the alcohol helped to deaden the effect.

We headed towards South William Street to find a quiet place. As we sat on the steps at the front of a shop, I could feel the swelling around my eye getting bigger and bigger. "Is it very noticeable, Harry?" I asked.

"Yeah, it's getting pretty obvious," he replied.

"How on earth am I going to get this money for Bobby?" I asked.

"Well, you better get it by next week or you're in big trouble," said Harry.

We spent the next hour or so racking our brains but couldn't find a solution. We *did* decide what story to tell my dad. I gave Harry ten wraps of speed to sell for me, with strict instructions to give the money from the sale directly to Bobby. I hopped into a taxi and sped home to Rathfarnham. I asked the taxi-driver to stop down the road from my house. As I walked towards the house I kept thinking, "How will I put this . . . will he swallow it?" There were no lights on. I hoped that everybody would be asleep. I opened the front door gently. I turned on the light and had a good look at my face in the oval mirror in the hallway. It wasn't a pretty sight. The left side of my face was horribly swollen, my eyes were bloodshot, bruising was beginning to show under the left eye. I heard my dad's bedroom door open. I rushed into the kitchen to get some ice for my face. As I heard my dad's footsteps coming down the stairs, my heart began to race, my brain went into overtime.

He came into the kitchen looking tired and exhausted.

"Where have you been, Julian? Do you realise what time it is?" he asked.

"I was with Harry, down in the Yellow House for a few pints," I said, turning around to face him.

"What happened to your face, Julian?" he asked in horror.

"We were leaving the Yellow House. Harry decided to walk up part of the way with me. We got to the Tuning Fork and a gang of about six guys crossed the road and started boxing and kicking us," I lied. What a load of old codswallop. I knew he wasn't going to buy this one, but it was the best that Harry and I could come up with.

"And did Harry get as bad a beating as you?" he asked.

"No, I think they were out to get me," I said.

"And did Harry just stand by and watch?" he asked.

"No, it just happened so fast. Don't you believe me?" I asked.

"No. I don't believe you," he said.

"Well that's what happened. I can't help it if you don't believe me," I said.

At this point I was on the verge of spilling my guts and telling him the whole truth. But Harry and I had already made up this story, so I was sticking to it. I couldn't tell him the real story because I didn't know how he would handle it, how he would react if he knew I owed someone £400 for drugs. And I was scared about what could happen if I told him who did this to me. I had a mental image of us tearing down to Stockton's apartment in the car. No, better just stick to the story.

"I thought you'd no money, Julian. How did you pay for the drinks?" he asked.

"Harry got paid today so he treated me to a couple of pints," I said.

"You've had more than a couple of pints, Julian. Now, I'll ask you once again, what really happened?" He wasn't buying any of this.

"I told you, Dad, we were attacked on the way home from the Yellow House," I insisted.

"Come into the lounge, Julian, and sit down for a moment," he said.

This is going to be a long interrogation I thought to myself, as I tried to act as sober as possible.

"Do you realise how lucky you are to have your eye, Julian? Another fraction of an inch and you'd have lost it," he said.

"Well it wasn't my fault, Dad, we were attacked," I said.

"I think you know who did this to you, Julian, and

I don't think it happened on the way back from the Yellow House," he said.

"I'm sorry, Dad, but that's the way it happened," I pleaded.

"Well, then you don't mind if I ring Harry to confirm all of this?" he asked.

"It's very late, but you can ring him if you like," I said.

He sat there for a moment. Then he said, "So you've no money with you now, Julian?"

"I've got about eighty pence bus fare," I said.

"OK. Take off your jacket," he said.

"What for?" I objected.

"Just take off your jacket, Julian," he said sternly.

"This is ridiculous." But I took my jacket off.

"Now let's see if you have any money in the pockets."

I squirmed.

"So what's this, Julian?" He took a twenty pound note out of my pocket.

"That's Harry's money. He asked me to mind it for him," I said.

"But I told you many times before, you're not allowed to mind money for anyone," he said.

"Yes, but I forgot," I offered feebly.

"Stand up, Julian," he said.

"Dad, for goodness sake. What's all this about?" I protested.

"Just stand up, Julian, and empty your pockets." I did. We found another twenty pound note and about four pounds in coins.

"Is all this Harry's money too?" he asked sarcastically.

"Yes, I'm minding it for him, so that he doesn't spend it," I said.

"Now, Julian, we're going to begin again with tonight's fairy story. Where were you?" he asked.

"I told you, Dad, I was in the Yellow House . . . " I started.

"Stop telling me lies!" he shouted. "I know you weren't in the Yellow House. I know that whoever did this to you, knew you. And I'm not resting until I get to the bottom of it. You can sleep on it tonight, Julian, but in the morning we'll be making a lot of phone calls. I'm sorry about your face but, until you start telling me the truth about this whole incident, I have no sympathy for you," he said.

I was in a state of semi-shock, but I realised that this was the end of the tall stories . . . he meant business.

"Get some sleep now, Julian. I'll call you in the morning, and then we'll sort this out. I think we'll need to call into the hospital to have your face examined. Maybe we'll drop down to the doctor in the morning," he said.

CHAPTER SEVEN

THE MORNING AFTER

The next morning I was woken up by my dad coming into my room. He asked how I felt. I told him I felt really bad.

"We'll have to get that eye seen to today, Julian. It looks dreadful," he said.

"Yeah, OK. I have to meet Mam at half eleven," I replied.

"Well then, why don't you have some breakfast? I'll drop you in to see Yvonne and then we'll go to St Vincent's Hospital. We have to have it looked at," he suggested.

"Yeah, sure, but I don't feel like having any breakfast. I can hardly move my mouth," I said.

When my dad left the room I got up and went into

the bathroom to have a look at my face. It was a lot worse than I expected. My left eye was practically shut, completely bloodshot. The left side of my face was swollen and purple in colour. I looked a sight. I got dressed and went downstairs.

The look of shock on Marina's face was something else.

"Oh you poor old thing, Julian. How do you feel?" she asked, giving me a hug.

"Sore," I replied.

"Let me have a closer look, Julian. My goodness, you were lucky you didn't lose your eye. Gerry, you'll definitely have to bring him to the hospital with that," she said.

"I am. He'd already arranged to meet Yvonne this morning so I'm dropping him in, and then we'll go to St Vincent's," said Dad.

We left to meet my mother. This was a meeting that I was not looking forward to. What a place she chose to meet . . . outside the police station in Pearse Street! I was dreading it. I knew the line of questioning would be a repeat of last night's episode with Dad. To make matters worse, my cousin, whom I hadn't seen for seven years, was home from Australia. My mother was bringing him with her today to meet me. I knew that she would be thoroughly ashamed of me when she saw the state of my face.

It was raining heavily as we pulled in at the police station in front of Mam's car. Dad got out and went back to speak with Yvonne for a moment. A couple of minutes later I saw Mam step out of her car. She was impeccably dressed as usual in a smart beige coat, her blonde hair was perfectly styled. But she had a fierce expression on her face as she and Dad came back towards our car. Oh no, here she comes . . . World War Three is about to commence.

"Merciful hour, Julian! What happened to you?" she said.

"I just got beaten up," I said, defensively.

"Let me look at it . . . oh, Julian, you're lucky you didn't lose your eye. Who did this to you? Julian, if I find out who did this to you, they better watch out . . . they'll never walk again," she said, shaking with rage.

"I don't know who did it, Mam. We were jumped on on the way home," I said.

"Oh, I suppose your friend Harry was with you," she said sarcastically.

"Yes, he was," I replied.

"And did he get as bad a beating?" she asked.

"No, not really," I said.

"Of course he didn't, because you know who it was, Julian . . . I know you do," she insisted.

"I don't!"

"What do you think, Gerry? I think this is a cock and bull story," she said.

"I think so too, but we're going to get to the bottom of it," said Dad.

"I'm damn sure we're going to get to the bottom of it," Mam said.

"We're going to the hospital now to have his face seen to," said Dad.

"Maybe we shouldn't bother, Julian? Maybe we shouldn't be worrying ourselves sick about your welfare? We should just let you hang around with those wasters. Why should we care if you don't care?" she continued.

"I *do* care," I interrupted.

"If poor Heidi was alive to see you today, Julian. You broke that poor woman's heart, and she spoiled you rotten. She had her doubts about Harry and all the rest of those so-called friends you're hanging around with," she said.

I wanted to tell her to shut up. I felt bad enough about the whole incident without her putting me down. Bringing up Heidi was the last straw. As she leaned forward to put her hand on my shoulder, I moved away. I couldn't look at her. She and Dad spoke outside the car for a few moments. My cousin, Ross, was in the passenger seat of her car. I'm sure he wondered what was happening.

"I think she was upset, Julian," said Dad sarcastically when he returned to the car.

"Not half," I replied.

"Well, we're going to get to the bottom of it, Julian," he said.

I didn't bother to reply. My head was aching, my eye was practically closed, and my face felt as if it had been run over by a steam-roller. I'd never felt so physically, emotionally and mentally drained in my entire life.

The waiting room in the hospital was half full of patients when we arrived. I had visions of being there for hours. The smell of the hospital did nothing for my sick stomach. We spent the next four hours drinking hot coffee and hot chocolate, and reading every magazine in the place. Eventually I was seen by the doctor. I had to be X-rayed. There was a slight fracture to my cheekbone, severe bruising and swelling to the eye and surrounding area. He prescribed some anti-inflammatory pills for me to take. It was ironic . . . the pills that he prescribed looked exactly like Ecstasy tablets.

When we got home I went straight up to my room and got into bed. It couldn't get any worse. As I lay in my bed I started crying. Rock bottom. Marina came into my room. She gave me hug and said, "Don't worry, Julian, I love you."

It was exactly what I needed at that moment. I must have drifted off because the next thing I remember was being called to the phone. As I came down the stairs to the phone, Tim, Jessica and Colin came out of their bedrooms to have a look at my face. I tried to avoid the astonished looks on their faces.

"Hi, Mam," I said.

"How's your face, Julian?" she asked. Her tone of voice was a lot different from that morning.

"Not too bad. I have a slight fracture of my cheekbone, and he gave me some anti-inflammatory pills for the swelling," I said.

"I'm sorry for some of the things I said to you this morning, Julian, but I was absolutely shocked when I saw the state of your face," she said.

"Yeah, I know," I said.

"If I didn't care I wouldn't be so upset," she said.

"Yeah, I know," I said.

"Listen, would you like to come over and stay with

me for a few days until all of this dies down a bit?" she asked. Mam lived over in Chapelizod.

"Yeah, that would be fine. I'd like that," I said.

"Well, what if I call over to pick you up at about lunchtime tomorrow?" she asked.

"Yeah, that's fine," I replied.

"OK. Don't forget to pack some extra clothes and socks and things," she said.

I was in a daze for the rest of the evening. I was taking pain-killers as well as the anti-inflammatory pills. My dad didn't start any more interrogating that night but he said we would have to discuss it all in great detail at the end of the week, after my few days in Mam's. The next four days were like the lull before the storm. I escaped to the safety of Mam's. I was away from the scene. I was delighted to be out of the house. It was a chance to relax and recuperate.

Whenever I'm staying there Mam is at my beck and call. Not because I want her to be, but because she likes to make a fuss of me. I sat down on the couch and everything was served to me.

Mam's house is really cosy. One of just ten houses situated in a tiny little cul-de-sac. The front room is a pale peach colour, and the suite of furniture is lovely and soft. Panelled glass doors divide the sitting-room and kitchen, and the lighting in the front room is subdued. A permanent aroma of oriental and eastern spices wafts from her kitchen. Toto, the dog, is an English terrier who marches around the house as if he owns it.

MARY CANTWELL LYNCH

I decided to get in contact with my counsellor. Hopefully she would be able to help me sort out the mess.

"Hello, Mary, it's Julian here," I said.

"How are you, Julian? How are things?" she asked.

"Not too good, I'm afraid. In fact they're very bad," I said.

"Do you want to come and see me?" she asked.

"Yes, as soon as possible," I replied.

"Well, let's see now . . . how about eleven o'clock in the morning?" she suggested.

"That's fine, Mary. I'll see you tomorrow morning," I said.

The next morning I woke up with butterflies in my stomach. This was the day it would all come to the surface. The drugs, the dealing . . . everything. I had to make a clean breast of it.

I was frightened by the time I got to Mary's house. Mary was her usual friendly self.

"How are you?" she asked when she saw my eye.

"As you can see, I'm still alive . . . just," I replied.

"So tell me what happened." she said.

"I got a beating from quite a big chap," I said.

"Have you had it seen to by a doctor yet?" she asked.

"Yes, I was in St Vincent's Hospital the day after it happened," I said.

"And is there anything broken?" she asked.

"No, just a slight fracture, and heavy bruising," I said.

"Gosh, it looks dreadful, Julian. You're very lucky," she said.

I knew it was only a matter of time before the next question was asked.

"Why did you get the beating?" she asked.

"It's quite a complicated story, Mary," I said.

"It's about the drugs, isn't it?" she enquired.

"Yes, I owe £400 to a dealer," I said.

"How did this come about?" she asked.

"I was given E to sell and I messed up on the payments for them," I said.

"What do you mean, you 'messed up', Julian?" she asked.

"I was given a bag of E and it was stolen from me. A friend of mine then gave me another bag of E to sell, but with the money I made from the sale of this bag of E, I paid off the guy who gave me the first bag of E. So now I still owe the £400 to the guy who gave me the second bag of E, but it's already sold and the money has gone to pay the first guy. Now I've no E and no money. I suppose this all sounds very confusing?" I said.

"Well, a little, but I get the gist of it. What are you going to do?" she asked.

"I don't know, Mary. I'm really stuck at the moment," I said.

"Does your dad know?" she asked.

"No, I haven't told him. I haven't told anyone. You're the only one who knows," I said.

"I think it would be a good idea to tell your dad," she said.

"I don't know, Mary. I don't know how he'd react," I said.

"How do you think he'd react? Does he love you or hate you?" she asked.

"He loves me, I suppose," I said.

"Well then, tell him. He's not going to rip your head off," she said.

"That's what I'm afraid of," I said.

"Well, what other way are you going to deal with it?" she asked.

"I have money in an account, but it's difficult to get at it . . . it's a trust fund," I said.

We spent the next hour discussing various ways of dealing with the problem. But I realised that I'd have to tell my dad the whole story. I didn't want to do that. Mary suggested that she would contact my dad, and arrange a meeting between the three of us for the next day. I agreed. At least there would be somebody else with me when he got the bad news. Mary picked up the phone and started to dial my home number. The conversation they had was brief and civilised.

My dad collected me as usual. On the journey home I waited for the question, "Why does Mary want to meet the two of us tomorrow?" But he never asked.

The following morning I woke up in a cold sweat, my heart in my mouth. There was very little conversation that morning, even on the car journey over to Mary's house. When we arrived at her house you could feel the apprehension in the air. As they say, "You could cut the atmosphere with a knife." Mary helped us to feel at ease with trivial small talk.

Then she got down to business.

"Well, Gerry, your son's in a spot of trouble. Big trouble," she said.

"I gathered that by his swollen face," said Dad.

"I'm afraid it's the involvement with drugs again," she said.

"How serious is it?" asked Dad.

"Maybe you'd like to explain the situation, Julian?" asked Mary.

"Well, Dad, I got the beating because I owe £400 for drugs," I said. I was sort of waiting for the explosion.

"And how come you owe £400?" he asked.

"It's a long story, but the money is owed," I said.

"He has to pay the money by next week, or else they'll make sure he lands up in hospital," Mary interrupted.

"So who gave you the beating, Julian?" asked Dad.

"Billy Stockton," I replied.

"Who's Billy Stockton?" he asked.

"He's a friend of Bobby Doyle," I replied.

"Well that explains the number of phone calls from Bobby Doyle this week. But who do you owe the money to?" he asked.

"I owe it to Bobby," I said.

"So why did Billy Stockton beat you up?" he asked.

"I don't know. He's just a friend of Bobby's," I said.

"And how come it's £400 that you owe?" he asked.

"Bobby gave me a bag of E to sell, but it was stolen from me," I said.

"And who stole it from you?" asked Dad.

"Frank Ryan stole it from me outside the club a few weeks ago," I said.

"Well why don't they go after Frank Ryan for the money?" suggested Dad.

"It's not as straightforward as that. But the main concern now is for Julian's safety. Somehow the money has to be paid, or else Julian gets a worse beating," said Mary.

"Well don't you worry about it, Julian, we'll sort it out. But I won't pay any money for drugs . . . not even if it was only five pounds. I don't know yet exactly how we're going to handle this, but we will handle it," he said.

He was so serious, it scared me. The look on his face said, "We're going to get these guys." It frightened me.

On the way home I was relieved by my dad's reaction to the whole thing, but I was scared that he was SO ADAMANT about not paying the money. His mind was obviously racing, and he was thinking out loud.

"Maybe there'll be quite a few people ending up in hospital this weekend," he said.

"What do you mean?" I asked.

"Well, nobody gives my son a beating like that and gets away with it," he said.

This was very pleasant to my ears . . . I started to visualise Stockton being beaten up. But it didn't help the fear. These guys would still be after their money.

INVESTIGATIONS AND PHONE CALLS

The following day my dad *did* begin to handle it. He sat me down in the front room and discussed his plan with me. It was like the incident room in the detective unit of the police force.

"Let's begin at the very beginning of this, Julian. If you want me to help you get out of this mess, you need to help me. Now, who do you owe the money to?" he asked.

"I owe it to Bobby Doyle," I answered. I realised that he meant business. I didn't have a choice. I had to tell him everything.

"What's Bobby's phone number?" he asked.

I gave him the number. "Please don't tell his mother, Dad, because she'll only kill him."

"Does his father know about his drug dealing?" he asked.

"Of course not. His parents don't know diddly squat," I said.

"What do you mean?" asked Dad.

"They don't even know that he takes drugs," I said.

"And who supplied him?" he asked.

"I honestly don't know, Dad," I replied.

"Well, we have to find out who's supplying him . . . and we will," he continued.

"Well, I don't know who it is," I answered.

"Who would know who supplies him?" he asked.

"Only Bobby," I answered.

"Well then I need to talk with Bobby first so I'll call his parents today," he said.

"He won't tell you a thing, Dad," I said.

"We'll see how much he tells after his parents are alerted to his conduct," he said.

I couldn't believe that he was actually going to contact Bobby's parents and expose the whole thing.

"Now where does this guy Frank Ryan fit into the picture?" asked Dad.

"He's nothing to do with it, except that he stole the bag of E from me," I said.

"Which caused the shortfall in cash in the first place," said Dad.

"Yes, but he's got nothing to do with Bobby," I said.

"There's no chance that it was set up for him to rob you?" asked Dad.

"No, definitely not. Bobby's not like that," I replied.

"You don't know what any of these guys are really like, Julian, until the chips are down. It's all about money . . . just money," he said.

"Anyway, I don't know where Ryan lives, and I don't have a number for him," I replied.

"Somebody must know where he lives, or have his phone number," said Dad.

"Maybe Tom would know," I replied.

"Who's Tom?" asked Dad.

"He hangs around with the Monkstown gang," I replied.

"Well let's ring Tom, then," said Dad.

"I don't have Tom's phone number, but I think John McKenna might have it," I said.

"And who's John McKenna?" asked Dad, beginning to sound a bit exasperated.

"He also hangs around Monkstown," I said.

"Do you have his number?" asked Dad.

"No, but Paul Hatton would have it," I said.

"OK. Let's ring Paul Hatton and get John McKenna's number," he said.

I went out and rang Paul, who gave me John

McKenna's number. I rang John McKenna and eventually got Tom's number. However, it was a little bit more difficult to get Frank Ryan's number from Tom. He was extremely reluctant to give it to me because he knew what Ryan had done to me. He made me swear that I wouldn't say where I got the number and eventually, after much persuading, he gave me Ryan's number.

"Now we're beginning to put the picture together, Julian. We've got Bobby's number and Ryan's number, but we're still missing Stockton's number," he said.

"I haven't a clue about Stockton's number," I said.

"Well, we'll get that from Bobby," said Dad.

"What are you going to do now, Dad?" I asked.

"I'm going to sort it all out before the day's over," he said with conviction.

I knew by the way that he said it, that he meant it. I dreaded the consequences. I couldn't imagine Bobby's reaction . . . not to mention his parents'! As for contacting Ryan and Stockton . . . I didn't even want to think about it. Where was it all going to end?

CHAPTER EIGHT

by Gerry Madigan

Keeping track of Julian's movements was an arduous task. But at least I was beginning to introduce some constants into a sea of variables. I knew he was with Mary Cantwell Lynch for his regular counselling sessions because I drove him there. I knew where he was when he was in the house, and I knew whom he spoke to on the telephone because I still recorded most of the conversations. And I knew that everything wasn't going as smoothly as I had hoped. I couldn't keep him under house arrest forever. I could see that he was quite agitated and frustrated.

The problem with trying to monitor your son's movements twenty-four hours a day is that you begin to feel like a spy. But I had to put those feelings aside. Yes, I was spying on my son, but that was necessary to save his life. I have always had an absolute abhorrence of drugs and those who ply this evil trade. I have always dreaded the very thought of my son becoming embroiled in that awful drug culture. Even though I was assured that he wasn't into drugs in a big way, I was vigilant. If that meant becoming a spy, then so be it . . . I would be a spy.

In the past, when I read the headlines about drug abuse or drug overdose, my interest was almost clinical. But suddenly these headlines jumped out of the newspapers at me. I couldn't believe the number of Ecstasy-related deaths.

We still had the problem of him staying overnight with friends without first consulting me. This was the most agonising period of the awful nightmare.

"What's the matter, Gerry?" asked Marina, as I jumped out of bed in the middle of the night.

"Just checking . . . I thought that was Julian at the door." I pulled back the curtain to look out the window.

"It's three o'clock in the morning, Gerry. Did you check his room?" she asked.

"I checked it at two o'clock and he wasn't in it then. I'll check again," I said.

This anxiety had become part of our normal existence. Disrupted sleep, worrying about his whereabouts, was he OK . . . It began to take its toll on my health. I found it difficult to function properly. My nerves were on edge. I became intolerant. Something had to give.

I laid down strict ground rules for Julian. But I knew that he was still seeing some of the gang. It was impossible to be his permanent shadow. There were times when he had to go into town or to work. I was sure he was meeting them then.

I will never forget the evening of Sunday 4th December 1994. Julian said that he was only going down the road to a friend's house, he would be back at about 10.30 p.m. As long as he stayed in the area I was happy enough. But he still hadn't arrived home by midnight. I checked the neighbour's house where he said he was going, but they hadn't seen him all night. I didn't sleep a wink that night. I twisted and turned, listening for the key in the door, waiting for the phone to ring . . . wondering, and fearing the worst.

Suddenly I heard the sound of a key in the door. Thank goodness he's home safe, I thought. As I went downstairs and walked into the kitchen, I was determined that this carry-on had to stop right now! What a sight greeted me. His poor face.

"What happened to your face, Julian?" I asked in horror.

"We were leaving the Yellow House . . . " he started.

I knew from the minute he opened his mouth that he was lying. This was no random beating. His face was disfigured, puffed out, turning black and blue. His eye was beginning to close from the swelling. I wanted to hug him, I wanted to give him a good shaking, I wanted him to come to his senses, I wanted to kill whoever did this to him. I wanted this madness to stop!

"OK. Take off your jacket, Julian," I said, and proceeded to search it.

"This is ridiculous," he protested.

The rest of our conversation that night set the scene for what was going to happen over the next few weeks. I told him that I was going to get to the bottom of it, find out who had beaten him up, expose the whole thing, contact parents. I also let him know that his movements would be severely restricted from now on. I went to bed and spent the rest of the night throwing it all around in my head, trying to quell the anger that kept swelling up inside me. I couldn't get the image of Julian's disfigured face out of my mind.

Before Julian eventually surfaced the next morning, I began my own investigation into the matter. My first phone call was to Harry. Obviously they had collaborated on the story because I got exactly the same story from Harry. It was too perfect. When I pressed him for more information he was far too vague. Harry knew who had done this to Julian . . . and I was going to find out who that was.

I brought Julian in to meet Yvonne the next morning. It wasn't a pleasant meeting. I'd never seen Julian at such a low ebb. We went to the hospital. The waiting around did nothing to lift his spirits. He looked wretched, sounded awful. He wanted to get it all over with and go home to bed. When we got home he went straight up to his bedroom. Yvonne rang later in the evening and invited him over to her house for a few days to let the dust settle. He stayed with her for a few days. During that few days the phone never stopped ringing for Julian. When he came back from Yvonne's he was rested. But the worried look on his face spoke volumes. I meant to talk to him at length the next morning.

However, I had to go out that morning and, when I got back, Marina told me that Julian had gone over to meet Mary Cantwell Lynch.

"That's strange. He didn't have an appointment for today," I said.

"I know but I think he phoned her as soon as he got up," said Marina.

Suddenly the phone rang.

"That's Mary Cantwell Lynch for you, Gerry," said Marina.

"Hello, Mary," I said.

"Hello, Gerry. I have Julian here with me . . . not looking or feeling the best," she said.

"Yes, he's in pretty poor shape," I agreed.

"I think we need to meet, Gerry, the three of us together," she said.

"That's fine with me, Mary. When have you got in mind?" I asked.

"As soon as possible. What about tomorrow morning at 10.30?" she suggested.

"Sure. That's great. Is Julian finished for today?" I asked.

"Yes he is," she replied.

"OK. Just tell him I'll be over in ten minutes to collect him," I said.

Our meeting with Mary next morning was an eye-opener. I *knew* that he had to have known who had hit him and it was a relief to hear that I was right in my hunch.

But his face went white when I said that I wouldn't pay any money to a drug dealer. When we came home the real investigation started. I was determined to get to the bottom of this, to finish this saga by exposing as many of the people as possible.

As Julian answered my questions, I started fitting the pieces of the jigsaw together. It was quite a complicated network of events.

"Let me get the story straight, Julian. You bought some Ecstasy from Jacko on credit. That Ecstasy was then stolen from you by Frank Ryan. You subsequently got more Ecstasy from Bobby, also on credit, which you sold. But you paid Jacko with the proceeds from the sale of Bobby's Ecstasy. Now you still owe Bobby for his Ecstasy, and that's why Billy Stockton beat you up. Have I got it right?" I asked.

"Yes, that's it," said Julian.

"Now I need phone numbers for Frank Ryan, Bobby Doyle and Billy Stockton," I said.

"I don't have a number for Frank Ryan or for Billy Stockton. I have Bobby's number," he said.

"OK. Who would have a number for Frank Ryan and Billy Stockton?" I asked.

Eventually we were able to find a telephone number for Ryan, but no luck with Stockton's number. But, now that I had the story straight and in sequence, I could start doing something about this mess. I wasn't quite sure exactly how I was going to do it, but I was going to do something.

As I mulled over the details of the incident, the phone rang.

"Hello. Would Julian be there please?"

"May I say who's calling?" I asked.

"Yes. Tell him it's Bobby."

My heart pounded, my hand trembled. Relax, calm yourself. Don't say anything. Don't blow it now, I told myself. Suddenly I found myself speaking to him.

"I know why you're ringing Julian. It's because he owes you £400 for drugs. Isn't it?" I asked.

Silence.

"I know that you got Billy Stockton to beat him up because he owes you this money. Does your father know about your drug dealing?" I asked.

"No . . . I mean . . . Look I'm quite prepared to forget all about the money. I knew nothing about Stockton beating him . . . I had nothing to do with that . . . I . . . "

"Well I won't forget about the money or the beating, Bobby. And when I'm finished with you, you'll never forget about this whole thing. Is your father at home?" I asked.

"Eh . . . no, he's not," he answered.

"Will he be at home this evening?" I asked.

"No, I don't think he'll be home until tomorrow." His voice quivered.

"Well tell your father that I'll be over to your house tomorrow evening at eight o'clock. Tell him he better be there, and you better be there also. I'll probably have my solicitor with me," I said.

Silence.

I had to sit down. My hands were shaking, my heart was pounding, and I was trembling. I'd started the ball rolling, I had to keep it rolling.

The telephone conversation stayed in my head all day and, in the early evening, I decided to call Bobby's house and check if his father was home. This time I would be more composed because I knew what I was going to say.

"Hello. Could I speak with Mr Doyle, please?" I asked.

"Yes. This is David Doyle speaking," came the reply.

"Hello, David. My name is Gerry Madigan, Julian Madigan's father," I said.

"Oh yes, I know Julian. How can I help you?" he asked.

"I hate to put this bluntly, but do you know that your son is a drug dealer?" I asked.

"I beg your pardon? I don't understand . . . " he answered.

"I'm sorry to be the bearer of such bad tidings, but

Julian is also involved. However, because of a deal he was doing with your son Bobby, he got a severe beating from Billy Stockton the other night," I said.

"I know Billy Stockton. But are you saying that Bobby was actually *selling* drugs?" he asked.

"Yes. They're all involved in it. Bobby sold some Ecstasy to Julian and, because Julian didn't pay Bobby for it, he was beaten up by Stockton," I said.

"Are you sure about all this? I mean . . . this is dreadful. I'm absolutely shocked. I'm sorry about this but I really don't know what's happening . . . " he continued.

"Well I'm sorry too, and I'm more than shocked at this stage. Is Bobby at home?" I asked.

"No. In fact I just met him as I came home. He was rushing out to meet somebody, I barely spoke to him. But I can assure you I *will* speak with him when he comes home tonight. What do you suggest we do about this?" he asked.

"Well I was anxious to speak with you first to alert you to the facts. I think that if we can expose what's going on we can possibly stop it. I think we should meet and discuss it anyway," I suggested.

"By all means. When did you have in mind?" he asked.

"Could I call over to your house tomorrow evening?" I asked.

"Yes, of course. I'll make sure that Bobby is here," he said.

"Would nine o'clock be convenient?" I asked.

"Fine. I look forward to seeing you then," he said.

As I finished the conversation I sighed with relief. At least he hadn't overreacted or become defensive or protective about it. He sounded pleasant and co-operative. But I still didn't know how we were going to handle the situation. As I was thinking about this later that evening, Mr Doyle rang back.

"Hello, Gerry. Sorry for interrupting you, but I've been talking to Bobby, and I think we should meet immediately. He's admitted dabbling with Ecstasy, and I think we should address this as soon as possible. Would you like me to call over to meet you this evening?" he asked.

"Not at all. There's not much that we can do tonight that can't be done tomorrow night. I think we can leave the original arrangement stand," I said.

"OK. I needn't tell you my wife is in a state of shock. But we're relieved about one thing, and that is the fact that he doesn't touch the stuff himself. We've been talking with him all evening, and he's admitted that he did sell a few tablets, but he has never taken the stuff himself," he said.

I didn't want to disillusion the man. He was suffering enough.

"Well let's discuss it all tomorrow evening," I said.

I came into the lounge and told Marina about the telephone conversation.

"The poor man. He's going to die when he hears the full story," she said.

"It'll be an interesting meeting tomorrow night," I said.

I had originally intended bringing Julian with me but I'm glad I didn't. He was staying with his mother, Yvonne for a few days. It would have been too confrontational if Julian had to face Bobby and listen to him give all the same excuses to his father that he had already given to me.

I rang the doorbell. I was a little apprehensive about how the meeting would go but I was determined to get to the bottom of this affair. I was pleasantly surprised by Mr Doyle's hospitable attitude and his genuine concern.

"Hello, Gerry. Thank you for coming over. It's a pity we have to meet under such shocking circumstances," he said.

"Indeed, but I'm afraid it's one of those distasteful chores that has to be done," I said.

He introduced me to his wife and his eldest son, and then we talked briefly about the situation before he brought Bobby in to face the firing squad. I had taken the liberty of inviting Liam Nicholson along in case I needed an independent witness, and in the hope that he could help Bobby in the same way that he helped Julian. He had joined us at this stage.

"Just before you bring Bobby in, David, I just want you to know that he does take drugs. He's actually more involved in drug abuse than Julian is," I said.

"Well he categorically denied any such drug abuse when we talked with him last night," his mother said.

"If he's taking drugs, let's try and find out now," said Mr Doyle, as he sent his eldest son off to get Bobby.

When Bobby walked into the room it was like looking at a carbon copy of Julian – without the bleached platinum hair. He had the same gaunt features and sunken eyes, and he wouldn't look at me. After the introductions Mr Doyle led off the discussion.

"Mr Madigan tells me that he knows for a fact that you do actually take drugs, Bobby. What have you got to say about that?" he asked.

"I told you before, Dad, I don't touch them myself. I only got involved that one time," he protested.

"You said you had nothing to do with the beating that Julian got, Bobby?" I asked.

"I heard about it, but I had nothing to do with it," he said.

"Where does Billy Stockton fit into the picture, Bobby?" I asked.

"I think he may be the supplier, Bobby, if I'm not mistaken," said Liam Nicholson.

Bobby said nothing.

"Well, Bobby?" said his father.

"Look, Bobby, we know the pattern here. We're familiar with this type of set-up, but if you had nothing to do with Julian's beating you need to come clean at this stage. Stockton *is* your supplier, isn't he?" said Liam.

"Now you just better start coming up with some answers, Bobby. Mr Nicholson and Mr Madigan are taking this matter very seriously, and so are we. What's going on between yourself and Billy Stockton?" said his mother, who was distraught at this point.

"Yes, he gave me the bag of E that I gave to Julian," he admitted.

"And then you kept putting pressure on Julian to come up with the money for it," I said.

"Were you being put under pressure from Stockton?" asked Liam.

"Well he needed to be paid for the stuff," said Bobby.

"And has Stockton been paid for it yet?" asked Mr Doyle.

"Yes, he's been paid," said Bobby, squirming.

"And where did you get the £400 to pay him?" asked his father.

"He borrowed it, David. But he had to give his record decks as security for the loan," I said.

Bobby glanced over at me with a look of disbelief on his face.

"Your good record decks, Bobby?" asked his father.

"I'll get them back, Dad. It was only a temporary loan," said Bobby.

"And from whom did you borrow this money?" asked his father.

"From Jimmy Fennell," said Bobby.

"Oh my goodness, Bobby. How dare you borrow money from Jimmy Fennell? You had no business borrowing, and you had no business giving your record decks as security," said Mrs Doyle. She was absolutely furious.

"I'm calling Fennell first thing in the morning,

Bobby, and you'll pay that money and get those record decks back," said his father.

Bobby was totally taken aback by this turn of events. He was beginning to crack under the intense interrogation.

"Perhaps if Bobby and I could have a little chat in private?" suggested Liam.

Both parents agreed. Liam and Bobby left the room.

"I'm absolutely devastated by all of this. I'm just beginning to handle the awful part about selling drugs, but to think that Bobby's actually taking drugs . . . oh this is dreadful," said Mrs Doyle.

"I'm baffled by the whole thing, Gerry. I can't believe that all of this was going on right under our noses. I'm very grateful to you for bringing this to our attention in the middle of trying to deal with your own problems with Julian," said David.

When Bobby and Liam came back, Liam started the conversation.

"I think at this stage Bobby needs to come clean with both of you if he wants to get out of this mess, and if he wants help in getting off drugs," said Liam to Mr and Mrs Doyle.

"Well, Bobby?" asked his mother.

"Yes, I have taken some Ecstasy as well as the little bit of hash," he admitted.

"And some acid too," added Liam.

"Yes, but I don't take much," he insisted.

"Well, *any* is too much in my book," I said.

"Absolutely," agreed his father.

"How are you coping with this, or rather how is Julian coping with this?" asked Mrs Doyle.

"He's attending a counsellor at present. But he's also forbidden to have anything to do with *any* of his so-called friends because most of them were involved with drugs," I said.

"Well let me tell you, there'll be very strict control on Bobby's movements from now on." She looked over at Bobby.

"Before we go, I'd like Stockton's address and phone number, Bobby," I said.

"I don't have his new address or phone number," said Bobby.

"Don't worry about that, Gerry. I'll have his address and phone number for you by tomorrow," said Mr Doyle.

As Liam and I left the Doyle house, I felt relieved that the first part of the job was over. I still had to decide how to bring everything to a successful conclusion, but at least I was making some progress, and the parents of one other Ecstasy user had been informed.

The next day I got a call from David Doyle with the address and phone number of Billy Stockton, as promised. I made my own enquiries to fill in the other missing link – the whereabouts of Frank Ryan. At least I had his phone number.

"Hello, I'm looking for Frank Ryan," I said.

"He's not here at the moment. I'm Mrs Ryan, his mother. Can I help you?" she asked.

"No, I just wanted to send some information to Frank about a sound engineering course he was enquiring about. Can I send it to him in the post?" I asked.

"Yes, of course. Do you have our address?" she asked.

"No, I don't," I replied.

She gave me her address. Now I had his phone number and his address. The jigsaw puzzle was complete. I didn't know what I was going to do with it, but at least I had all the relevant information.

We came up with a plan of action to help Julian extricate himself from the influence of his friends. The phone calls had rapidly increased in number since my visit to the Doyle's house. We decided that Julian would never answer the phone himself. I always said that he was out whenever anyone phoned for him.

Eventually we put the word out that he had gone to Australia to stay with his cousin for six months. This worked wonders . . . the phone calls stopped coming. Now it was only a matter of being careful about where he went, in case he was seen by any of these friends. He never ventured into town after he got the beating. I dropped him over to his regular sessions with Mary Cantwell Lynch. Having eliminated the distractions, he was now on the road to recovery.

This was going to be a long and difficult road. He had to give up so much, change so much, find a new direction. I had to try to involve him more in everyday family life. I had to monitor his behaviour, and maintain a healthy vigilance on where he went. This part wasn't too difficult because he wasn't inclined to go outside the front door. This was going to be a combined effort to get Julian back on track, to help him start living again.

CHAPTER NINE

CHURCH FUNCTION

Just before the Christmas of '94 my dad and Marina invited me down to one of the functions in the Church. They were both members of the Church of Jesus Christ of Latter-Day Saints (the Mormon Church). I was very apprehensive at first but I decided to go with them because I had nothing better to do. I used to attend an odd function in the Church when I was about thirteen, so I got to know a few people around my own age. They were always good fun, but Heidi had always told me before I went, "If they mention anything about religion, just say you're not interested."

When we arrived at the Church I was surprised to see the large number of cars in the car park. My dad had said that it wouldn't be too packed, but by the looks of things it was going to be very packed.

"Is this a large function, Dad?" I asked.

"Yes, it's the Christmas dinner," he replied.

"It's Christmas dinner, followed by a dance," explained Marina.

"What sort of food will there be?" I asked.

"The usual turkey and ham with the trimmings," he said.

When as we walked into the place I felt uncomfortable. People came up to me, shook my hand and asked how I was . . . long time no see, etc. I couldn't remember any of them. I wanted to run out of the place and wait in the car. We went into the main hall and sat down to dinner. Sure enough, turkey and ham with roast potatoes, carrots and brussels sprouts, followed by plum pudding and custard. I only ate the turkey and ham, because the rest of the food was not as hot as I like it . . . I'm very fussy about my food.

When the dinner was finished there was a dance. My dad and a few of his Church friends supplied the music. Country music, sixties music, and nineties middle-of-the-road material. The only way I knew how to enjoy myself at a dance was by necking a few pills and dancing with lovely looking girls. *This* was totally different. No flashing laser lights, pumping loud music, dancers going crazy.

The thing that struck me about that night was the genuine friendliness of the people. Even though I didn't really like the dinner, I did enjoy myself. I didn't join in the conversation at dinner, and I didn't make any effort to talk to anyone during the dancing either. But it was a good night – very different from my usual escapades.

CHRISTMAS AND COLD TURKEY

On Christmas Eve I was pretty bored. Some local guys invited me out for a few drinks. This was the first time I had been outside my house in a public place (besides the Church function) for a while. I told my dad that I would be back at ten o'clock. He wasn't too keen on me going out to the pub.

"You're to be home at ten o'clock on the dot. Do you hear me, Julian?" he asked.

"Yes, Dad, I'll be home," I replied.

"It's Christmas Eve, Julian, and we want to go to bed early," he added.

"You mean I've to be home before Santa Claus comes?" I laughed as I went out the door.

We arrived at the pub at about eight o'clock and started buying rounds. I hadn't drunk for a while so my capacity was very low. After the fifth pint I began to feel the effects of the alcohol . . . I was well on my way. I ordered another one, and asked what time it was. A quarter past ten! My heart skipped a beat.

"Sorry, lads, I have to go," I said.

"Ah, stay for a little longer. It's Christmas Eve," said one of them.

"No, it's OK, lads. I'll see you over the Christmas," I said.

My pint arrived and I knocked it back. As I was walking home I saw my dad and Marina driving towards me. I'm dead, I thought to myself.

"Hi, Dad. Sorry I'm a bit late," I said in a slurred voice.

"Where were you, Julian? It's ten fifteen," he said.

"I was just down in the pub," I explained.

"I'll see you at home in a few minutes. Go straight home," he said, and drove off.

As I walked home I wondered why he was out in the car looking for me. I was only fifteen minutes late, which was brilliant by my normal standards . . . I used to be three days late!

"Julian, I thought you were trying to get your head

together after everything you've been through over the last few weeks?" said Dad.

"I am, Dad. I don't know what all the fuss is about. You said I could go out for a few drinks, and now, because I'm a bit late home, you're all uptight," I said.

"This is the first night you've been out since the beating up incident, Julian. And what happens? You can't even be trusted to come home on time!" he shouted.

"But, Dad, I was only down the road with a few of the local guys," I said.

"Marina and I called into the pub to see if you were there, and you weren't," he continued.

"Well then, I must have just left. You saw me walking up the road," I said.

"Maybe I should ring Billy Stockton and let him know that you're still around?" he said.

This was really going over the top, I thought. Was he mad in the head? Talk about overreacting, this was ridiculous. The very thought of that suggestion sent a shiver up my spine.

"Dad, I'm sorry I'm late home. I didn't realise the time but, as soon as I did, I finished my drink and left," I said.

"Julian, do you not understand what we've all been through? You can't go out for drinks like that and then arrive home late. I don't know who's after you, or what's happening. I'm only concerned about your welfare. You've also had more than a couple of pints," he said.

"Well it's Christmas Eve, Dad. Surely I'm entitled to do a little bit of celebrating?" I suggested.

"You obviously don't realise the danger that you could put yourself in by doing it, Julian. Anyway, let's make it a happy Christmas. I'm glad you're alive and healthy."

I was really surprised by the way my dad reacted to my being late, but the following morning I began to see his point of view. I was awoken by the sound of Tim getting dressed. My head was thumping like nobody's business. My mouth was as dry as a bone and I felt rotten. I think it was only the second time I had a hangover and I promised myself it would be the last. I strolled into the toilet in a semi-conscious state and, as I sat on the side of the bath, I broke out in a cold sweat. I started seeing stars. I felt like vomiting. I'd had this feeling before but only when I went overboard on hash, never with drink.

We all went downstairs to open our Christmas presents and that brought back memories of Heidi and Monaloe. It was so funny to watch little Jamie toddle over to the Christmas tree, pick up a present and wait for Marina to tell her what to do . . . She would then deliver the present to the appropriate person and watch them with great excitement as they opened their present. Afterwards, Marina, Dad and the kids went off to visit Marina's brother, Eugene, and his family. I decided that it would be better for me to stay at home. I went back to bed for a while to sleep off the hangover. For the first Christmas in a couple of years I felt really good inside. I wasn't hiding anything, I was myself, and I had something good to look forward to . . . life.

CHAPTER TEN

SOCIAL LIFE AND LIFESTYLE

On the 1st of January '95 I made some New Year's resolutions. My lifestyle had changed dramatically in a short period of time. The only thing I ever looked forward to was the weekends . . . Thursday to Sunday. Now a Friday night was no different from a Monday night or a Tuesday night. I had no social life. Ecstasy was everywhere. I couldn't meet my friends because nearly all of them were on Ecstasy. I couldn't go to the clubs and raves because they were full of Ecstasy. I would probably meet some of my old "friends" there. I couldn't go into town for fear of meeting Stockton or some other guys looking for money which I owed. The world could have collapsed outside my front door and it wouldn't have mattered to me. I had never spent more than a few hours in the house, and now I lived inside the house practically twenty-four hours a day.

For the first few weeks after giving up drugs, my days were very lazy. I found it difficult to sleep and, when I finally got up out of bed at about eleven o'clock, I was still exhausted. I would wander down the stairs into the kitchen to have some breakfast. Then I would plonk myself in front of the television and watch a video as I ate my breakfast. I spent most of the time in front of the TV. I didn't want to do anything else. I would doze off in the sitting-room and my dad would wake me for dinner.

I began to get a lot closer to the rest of the family. Before this I barely knew Tim, Jessica and Colin. As far as I was concerned they were three young annoying kids who got on my nerves. Suddenly I realised they were small human beings. Thirteen-year-old Jessica was normal for her age . . . heavily into Take That, and fancying boys. Colin, like all eleven year olds, was a football fanatic. I didn't hold it against him that he supported Aston Villa . . . sure he was only young. Tim, at fifteen, was obsessed with wrestling. If he had his way we'd all be watching WWF wrestling on television twenty-four hours a day. Jamie was eighteen months at the time. I began to play with her and listen to her garbled language. It made me feel good inside every time I played with Jamie. I'd stop and think how lucky I was to have broken out of the drug scene, that someday I could have a child of my own. I was beginning to laugh in the house again. I didn't have the downers that I usually had from the after-effects of the drugs. Marina would often point out to me that I was a different person now. She could communicate with me. She was only getting to know the real Julian now.

"Is this the same person of a few months ago?" she asked.

"Yes, it's the new model. There've been a few improvements. What do you think?" I laughed.

"I think it's brilliant to see a smile on your face and a fresh look about you," she said.

"Well you see I've been trying to perfect those smiles for the last couple of years, and it's only recently that I've mastered them," I said.

"You're not at all like the Julian of a few months ago. You laugh, you smile, and you actually talk to people," she said.

After a few lethargic weeks, my dad began to encourage me to get up early in the morning. He reminded me about the mornings that we used to get up at 6.30 and go to Westwood Health Club for our run, workout and squash. I couldn't even begin to think about that. I was light years away from it. But Dad insisted. He put a stop to late night TV. I had to put my life back together again piece by piece. I knew I couldn't jump in at the deep end and pretend that nothing had happened, but I did start getting up in the mornings for the odd short run around the block.

Slowly but surely my life was beginning to become more stabilised. I got up and went to bed at reasonable times. I was totally out of shape physically, mentally and emotionally. But I realised that I had to do something to get myself back into shape. I'd lost a lot of weight and muscle when I was taking Ecstasy. In fact I was quite scrawny. I was a new person. I needed a new body. At the beginning of the New Year my dad and I went into town and bought some weights. Going into town was a treat, but I had no idea what a kick I would get out of walking around the sports shop. I hadn't done this in years. Suddenly all my enthusiasm for sport flooded back. This was a different type of high for me . . . looking at the runners, trying them on . . . looking at the weights, deciding which ones to buy . . . the posters around the shop, the gear, everything. Hey, this is what I was into!

I felt a great sense of achievement as we paid for the weights. My dad went off to get the car and arrived back a few minutes later. We put the weights into the boot of the car, and then we headed off for a pizza to celebrate. As we drove home in the car I was delighted with my new purchases, but I was even more satisfied with myself. I was ready to become the new Julian Madigan.

It's over a year since I stopped using drugs . . . and what a year it's been. My recovery started off with a punch and then a visit to a hospital, so I don't think I can complain.

The things which have helped me through the last year have been the support from my family, the encouragement from my coach in the running club, the fellowship from my new friends in Church, and the concerned regular contact from Liam Nicholson. All of these things have contributed to my success in breaking away from the drug culture.

It's very much like trying to give up cigarettes. I've watched hundreds of my friends and relations making futile attempts to kick the smoking habit. That is because they don't *really* want to give them up. A little voice inside them which says, "Go on, have one . . . you don't really want to give them up", foils their attempt. Nobody can give up cigarettes unless they *really* want to.

The same thing applies to drugs. Nobody can give up drugs unless they really want to. All the scare-mongering about the dangers to health will not make someone give up drugs. More people die each year from nicotine-related disease than all other drugs put together.

I didn't have to deal with the physically addictive drugs like cocaine and heroin. But the social addiction of Ecstasy and hash is an incredibly strong force. People think that it's the drugs which are addictive, but in fact it's the culture. The friends, the atmosphere, the clubs and the parties. Those were the things that I was addicted to. The drugs enhance the enjoyment of all of these things to make them even more appealing. You can ask someone to give up the pleasure of puffing cigarettes. But we're talking about a different kind of pleasure when we talk about the buzz, the excitement, the happy family atmosphere, and the fun of the drug scene. In four years I don't think I missed a single weekend in town. I lived for those weekends. I was having fun!

The first two months after "The Incident" were the hardest. All my old friends kept ringing for me. I didn't answer the phone. The messages were relayed to me by Dad or Marina. But just hearing, "That was Harry looking for you again", would bring back memories of things we did together. These things weren't always drug related, but maybe things that we did in school. This was the difficult part, to drop people that I grew up with and had fun with before we all got involved with drugs. In many cases the drug culture destroys friendship.

A few of the local lads would call around to the door and ask me if I would smoke a couple of spliffs with them.

"All right, Madzer. Are you coming over to Mick's house for a few spliffs?"

"No, you're all right, lads," I replied.

"Aw c'mon, Madzer. Look, I've got a big lump of Rocky," said one of them.

Sure enough, they had about a quarter of hash, which is about thirty-five pounds worth.

"No thanks, lads. I'm not into that sort of stuff anymore. Thanks all the same," I said.

I was surprised that my first reaction to these requests was always no. However, the subconscious reaction was not as easily controlled. When I went to bed at night, after these incidents, I had dreams about my past . . . being in clubs, doing drugs, etc.

DROPPING FRIENDS

One of the hardest things I've ever done was to decide to cut all ties with the drug culture. That meant dropping all my friends who were involved in drugs in any way whatsoever. And *that* meant dropping most of the friends whom I had hung around with over the past four years.

When I talked to my counsellor the day I told all, she said that it would be hard to give up drugs and not be tempted, if I was still hanging around with friends who still did drugs. She also said that I should take a good look at my friends, and try to discover if they were *real* friends. Could they help me through this period? I didn't want to listen to her at first. I couldn't see why I had to drop my friends. It took me about four days to realise that, if I really wanted to get out of the drug scene for good, I would have to drop my friends and cut all connections with them. Believe me, it was hard to drop them, to try to forget people with whom I'd had such good times (and some bad times).

They didn't want to drop me. As soon as I decided to break away, the phone started to hop. There were about twenty calls a day from various groups of my friends. My dad and Marina were the only ones allowed to answer the phone. I never got to speak to any of them directly.

I lived in isolation for the next few months. I barely stepped outside my front door and, if I did, I never ventured further than a few hundred yards from the house. My dad seemed to think that he was forcing me to stay in, but I honestly didn't want to go outside for fear of any of my old friends seeing me. I had this ashamed feeling inside me because of ratting on people and what I'd done to Bobby. A part of me still lived in that drug culture . . . even though I was physically removed from it. To this day I wonder what they said about me then, and just how much hate they have for me now. Dad put the word out that I'd gone to stay with my cousin in Australia for six months. The phone calls eventually stopped. Whether they believed the story or not, it got them off my back.

Almost every day I came across something – music, conversation, situations that brought me back to the drug scene. The high. The thrill. But the flashbacks were frightening. When I heard a song . . . suddenly I'd remember where I was, what I was on, who I was with, and the euphoria I felt. Whenever I felt down, depressed or discouraged, all it took was the sound of the rave music to spark off that longing to be with my friends. I was lonely on that long road to recovery.

The first eight weeks were the hardest. Trying to get asleep early and trying to rise early were impossible. I don't remember much about this particular time, but my dad informed me that it was hard for me and for the rest of the family. There are huge blank areas when I try to remember that. Apparently I was just like a zombie. "Lights on, but nobody's home." I couldn't believe the sense of loneliness, even though my family were all around me. Waking up at midday, having something small to eat, sitting down to watch a film, dozing off, wandering about the house aimlessly. Yes, I was a zombie all right.

PHYSICAL FITNESS

Once I started to break out of that pattern, things began to happen. Without the drug culture there was a huge void that had to be filled. Sport came into my life again. I began to regain my health, and I concentrated all my efforts on getting back into physical shape.

When Liam Nicholson called he always gave me encouragement, support and advice. I always felt good after his visits. This was a guy who worked hard with other people who were on drugs, and yet he took the time to call in to see me and check on my progress. It was nice to know that there was somebody, besides my immediate family, who cared. I appreciated this concern which he had for me. On one of his visits he asked me had I any hobbies or sports.

"Did you have any hobbies or interests before you started into the drugs, Julian?" he asked.

"Yeah. I swam, and I also did a lot of athletics," I replied.

"Were you any good at them?" he asked.

"I wasn't too bad. I won a few medals here and there," I replied.

"Would you be interested in taking up running again?" he asked.

"I don't know. I might be," I replied.

"Well, if you do decide to take it up, just give me a ring and I'll introduce you to a friend of mine who has a running club quite close to here," he said.

I'd never had to do as much thinking as I did in those few weeks. Should I get back into running?

Would I ever be able to get back? What if my body just couldn't do it? I was lifeless right then . . . no energy whatsoever. How could I compare with others in the club? How could I muster up the enthusiasm again for competitive sport? My life was changing right before my eyes. The drug scene had taken up such a large part of my life and, now that it was gone, there was a large vacuum that had to be filled. Going back to running seemed to be an ideal solution to the problem. I had just given up cigarettes. My first step was to stop buying them. Automatically my consumption dropped because nobody else at home smoked, and I wasn't socialising. There must have been something inside of me that hated cigarettes, because the last one I had was in my mother's house. Everyone had gone to bed, and I was sleeping downstairs in the front room. I noticed a box of Benson & Hedges cigarettes on the mantelpiece. I took one out of the pack and lit up. The very first drag tasted awful. I didn't even inhale it, I just blew it out and stubbed the cigarette. How did I ever like them? Had my taste buds changed so much in four weeks? Now was as good a time as any to get back into training. By the time Liam got back to me, I had decided to go back to running.

"Well, Julian, did you think any more about the athletics?" said Liam.

"Yeah, I had a good think about it and I decided to give it a shot," I said.

"Good man, that's great news. I'll get in contact with my friend to find out what nights they train," he said.

"That would be great," I said.

"When I find out the times, I'll give you a ring, pick you up and bring you over to introduce you to him. How's that?" he asked.

"Thanks, that would be lovely," I said.

I can still remember the butterflies in my stomach on that Tuesday night before I went over to meet the coach at the club. The arrangement was for 6.00 p.m. on the Tuesday, so I was ready from 5.30 p.m. Unfortunately, Liam was late. I was twice as nervous by the time he came. I had mixed feelings. The fear of not knowing anyone at the club, and meeting new people. The excitement of starting off in a new direction. I have some idea of how an alcoholic must feel before he attends his first AA meeting, cold sober. For the previous four years I'd never had a problem going to raves and mixing with hundreds of people. We all had the same interests (drugs and dance), and we were all high on drugs. This was a different kettle of fish . . . no drugs or stimulants of any kind, just me. But if I ever wanted to get the high again that I used to get from sport, I would have to overcome my nervousness. If my position on a compass had been due north up to now, tonight I was heading due south.

"Are you ready to go, Julian?" Liam said in a hurried voice.

"Yeah, I'm ready," I replied.

"How are things, Marina?" he asked.

"Great. Best of luck tonight, Julian," she said.

As I hopped into the car, I felt almost sick with nerves. On the way over, Liam explained that this coach was excellent, and not to be nervous. His name was Eddie McDonagh. I'd never heard of him, but Liam assured me that he was fine. He was right.

I headed for the changing rooms, and then sat down on one of the side benches. Liam went into the hall to get Eddie. A couple of minutes later they both arrived back.

"This is Julian, Eddie," said Liam.

"How are you, Julian? What distances do you run?" he asked, shaking hands.

"I was a sprinter. I did mainly 100 and 200 metres. On an odd occasion I'd do a 400," I said.

"Come inside to the hall when you're ready, OK?" he said.

"Well, I'll leave you in his capable hands now, Julian," said Liam.

"Thanks very much, Liam. I really appreciate this," I said.

Suddenly I was on my own. I felt like a little boy on his first day at school. I took a deep breath and entered the hall. Kids, kids and more kids, that's all I saw, except for the coaches and trainers. Is there anybody here my age, or am I the oldest one here? I wondered.

Eddie called me over. "Do a few laps of the hall to get warmed up, Julian, and I'll talk to you in a minute."

I took off my top and did a couple of laps. I felt paranoid. I was sure that everybody in the place was looking at me and criticising. When I had finished doing the laps, Eddie asked me to do a few short sprints.

"Of course." I did them to the best of my ability.

"Not bad, Julian, but there's a bit of work to be done," he said.

I felt like an old rusty bucket that had been taken out of the shed to put out a fire. I was stiff and worn. My legs felt as if they were attached to a ball and chain, my lungs hadn't had this much exercise in a long time. It felt weird doing those short sprints. It brought back memories of a time a few years ago when I used to run and train regularly. Was I the same person who won those medals and trophies, or was I past it at nineteen years of age? To tell you the truth I *felt* past it, but something inside me told me to stick at it . . . I could get back on track, and I *would* get back on track. I knew that this was going to be one hell of an uphill battle. But, if I had been able to give up the drugs, surely I could manage it.

After the sprints I joined in the circuit training with the girls. I was the only male in the group, but that didn't make me feel too uncomfortable. The circuit involved lots of medicine ball drills, push-ups and sit-ups. My lungs felt as if they were going to collapse, even though I'd been off cigarettes now for *three weeks*. After the session I felt wrecked, drained.

Before I left, Eddie came up to me and told me that training would be Tuesdays, Wednesdays and Thursdays in the hall, and on Saturday and Sunday mornings in the local park. He advised me not to do more than three days a week at first, and then to slowly increase. I could hardly survive the first night. How on earth was I going to manage this? I thanked him, and then I headed home.

"Well, Jules, what was it like?" asked Marina.

"It was fine, but they were very young. I was probably the oldest," I replied.

"How do you feel after your first night's training?" asked Dad.

"You could say I feel tired, but I'm absolutely starving," I replied.

"Well you're bound to feel stiff and tired, Julian. Remember that you've been out of touch for about three years, so you'll need to ease back into it," he said.

"So when are you training next, Julian?" asked Marina.

"Saturday morning in the park, and then Tuesday and Thursday nights for the moment," I said.

I trained three days a week, and never missed a single session. This was February of 1995, and by May of that year I increased my training to six days a week. How I did it, I'll never know. The first few weeks were unbelievably hard. I remember going for a two-mile run . . . I thought my chest was going to burst, my throat was burning up, and I thought my shins were about to crack. But I wasn't giving up. This had to work. I focused on my training. Hail, rain or snow, I wouldn't miss it. The harder and tougher it got, the more I wanted. I tried to break the pain barrier by pushing myself to the limit and beyond. But I was training myself into the ground. By August of '95 my coach noticed that I was beginning to look very tired. Dad and Marina were also worried, and they suggested that I ease up a little. I ignored them. I was determined to get back in shape, no matter what. However, I didn't realise that my running times were beginning to decrease instead of increase. In May I ran the 100 metres in 11.20 seconds, and in August my times were up to 11.80 seconds. I got more and more sports injuries. My coach suggested that I visit a physiotherapist to have my legs checked out. I spent the next few days trying to find a good physiotherapist within easy reach of my house. It was also important that he or she wasn't too expensive, and that they specialised in sports injuries. Fortunately I found just the right guy, and my course of treatment began.

As I walked up the stairs in the modern premises where he had his clinic, I couldn't help noticing the pictures that hung on the wall of the stairway. A selection of high profile people from various sporting backgrounds. This guy must be OK, I thought.

"Hello, I'm Julian Madigan. I'm here to see Arnold Bluth," I said to the tall, dark-skinned gentleman.

"Ah yes, Julian. Come this way please." He led me into his surgery.

As he massaged my legs, he asked me about my training schedule.

"I'm training about six days a week at the moment," I said.

"What type of training?" he asked.

"Running. Sprints mostly," I said.

"Your muscles are very stiff and tired. That's why you're getting the injuries. You're suffering from chronic muscle fatigue in your legs, Julian, and that's due to over-training with insufficient recovery periods," he explained.

"I suppose this means taking a bit of a break?" I asked.

"Yes, you'll need a lot of rest, but you'll also need to watch your diet," he said.

"For my weight?" I asked in surprise.

"No, not for your weight. You need to replace a lot of magnesium and potassium in your muscles," he explained.

I left the physio's clinic feeling disappointed. I'd have to miss the last few races of the season. But I was glad that I had seen him and found out the problem. It explained why my times weren't improving, and why I felt so tired.

Since I'd joined the running club I'd made a lot of new friends and acquaintances who were a great help to me. I'd no other social life since I dropped all my old friends. The new friends took my mind off the drugs and my old way of life. When I think back I realise that this was an essential part of my recuperation, or should I say rehabilitation! Once I gave up the drugs, fags, and booze, and the lifestyle that went with it, there was an enormous gap that needed to be filled. Running and training filled that dangerous vacuum.

The coach, Eddie, was a great help. He often complimented me on my enthusiasm and drive. I got a real sense of belonging with this club when I attended the regular training sessions, and I realised that it wasn't all girls. Since I gave up drugs I hadn't felt part of anything besides the family. The group that I hung around with on the drug scene was like a little family. We all looked out for one another, even though we were all partners in crime. The same type of family atmosphere existed in the running club, but what we had in common was our healthy interest in sport, not drugs. Running was something I really loved doing, and it was a chance for me to get out of the house and do something on my own. There was a large selection of guys and girls of various age groups and different competitive levels. I made friends with many of the athletes around my own age, and I looked forward to travelling with the club to athletic meetings around the country. There was a fabulous atmosphere on the coach as we headed off to compete in national championships. It reminded me of my younger days (before drugs) when we set off to compete as a school team, only this time we were the guys at the back of the bus.

CHAPTER ELEVEN

SPIRITUAL DIMENSION

Religion came back into my life, only this time in a different form. I understood the need for religion in my life. When I was involved with drugs I had no interest in God or anything spiritual. My dad and my grandmother were very spiritual, but none of it rubbed off on me. But then I don't think anything rubbed off on me at that time. However, one summer's evening Peter, Danny and I were up near the forest in Cabinteely. We looked into this field and, as the summer mist set on the long golden grass, we saw an absolutely beautiful horse standing motionless in the middle of the field. A film of mist glistened on his back in the glow of the evening sun.

"And people say that there's no God," I said.

"There isn't any God. Jesus was just a wise man," said Peter.

Then it hit me. I believed in God and Jesus Christ, and these guys that I was hanging around with didn't believe in anything.

Once I started to get my life back on track in December of 1994, my dad encouraged me to start getting some spiritual direction into my life.

"What are your beliefs, Julian?" asked Dad.

"I believe in God," I replied.

"Do you have any sort of relationship with God?" he continued.

"How do you mean . . . praying and all that?" I asked.

"Well praying would be part of it, but to whom do you pray? Do you have any other way of worshipping or paying tribute to God?" he asked.

"Well I used to go to Mass occasionally," I replied.

"Now that you're trying to get your life in order, Julian, you should also try to develop your spiritual dimension," he said.

"Yeah, I suppose I should," I replied.

"Well you have to do something about it, because your spiritual dimension doesn't just suddenly happen . . . you have to make it happen," he said.

"Yeah, well I'll have to start doing something," I agreed.

"But what, Julian? Do you believe in the Catholic Church, or do you believe in any Church?" he asked.

"I'm not really sure right now," I replied.

"Then you should investigate the various beliefs, Julian, and find out for yourself what life is all about. I know what I believe in, but you have to find out for yourself. You need to start looking seriously at it. Why don't you take a look at what I believe in, and if you don't like that, then look at something else?" he suggested.

"Yeah, why not?" I replied.

I knew that it was something I should have done a long time ago, but now that I was making so much effort in every other direction in my life, it was time to find out what this spiritual dimension was all about. Heidi was a devout Catholic all her life. My dad had joined the Mormon Church in 1979. I really had nothing, because I'd stopped going to Mass, and I hadn't given religion any great thought for the past few years. Just before Christmas of '94 I set up an appointment to meet two missionary elders from the Church of Jesus Christ of Latter-Day Saints (the Mormon Church). Marina and the children were all active members of the Mormon Church.

A few days later Elder Conk and Elder Wilson called to the house. These guys were very well presented clean-cut young men and I instantly took a liking to them. They were around my own age, and had similar interests (apart from drugs!). We talked about sports and hobbies before they got down to presenting the gospel of Jesus Christ to me. Once a week these missionaries had a free day, called "P day", on which they would make preparations for the coming week, organise their laundry, and relax from the normal proselytising duties. They often invited me to join them on their P days at the National Basketball Arena to play basketball with them and other missionaries. In the group of twenty guys there were only three non-Americans, myself and two others. This was obvious as we were the last to be selected for basketball teams. I always had a good time with them. And I began to take a real interest in their Church. I started learning about new and exciting things. Questions which I always had, but were never answered, were being answered by these young men. They were jokers and messers, but behind it all I saw just how important the Church was to them. As our discussions continued, the Plan of Salvation put things firmly into perspective for me. I realised why the Church and the gospel were so important to these guys.

During one of the discussions the Elders told me about the three degrees of glory in the next life. "What are they?" I asked. They told me that there were three kingdoms in heaven – the Celestial, Terrestrial and Telestial Kingdoms. Which one you get to depends upon how well you live your life on this earth. "I want to spend the rest of my life in the Celestial Kingdom," I said.

"Then you need to live a good life, and strive to live by a celestial law," said Elder Conk.

This was beginning to make a lot of sense to me. I'd always understood that if you'd led a good life you'd get to heaven. But surely the person who leads a better life should be entitled to a better heaven? Would Mother Theresa of Calcutta and I end up in the same place?

At a Church function I was talking to a friend of mine who was a member of the Church. We discussed the importance of being a member of the Church, of getting baptised. My self-worth increased when I understood that I was actually a child of God. I had the potential to become perfect, to overcome all temptation. I could become a person of integrity and be an example to others, instead of justifying bad behaviour.

"I can't help it, that's the way I am," says the drunk.

"I didn't mean to do it. I just can't help myself," says the child abuser.

I learned about repentance from the Elders. When you do something wrong, you can either repent or justify your actions. But to say you just can't help it is not a justification, it's a cop out. I had a lot of repenting to do, and one of the important steps to true repentance is to stop doing it. "Go, and sin no more" – it's not true repentance if you keep on repeating the offence.

There was more to life than drugs. I realised that I could be better than I was. I had the freedom to make that choice. We have all been made in the image and likeness of our Heavenly Father and Jesus Christ, and we can aspire to be like them. We have been asked to be Christ-like, to strive to be perfect. When I realised all of these things, it didn't take me too long to decide to be baptised. I remember telling my dad on the way home from a friend's house.

"Dad, I've decided to get baptised," I said.

"That's great. When did you decide?" he asked.

"A couple of nights ago," I replied.

"So when is the date?"

"The 9th of February," I said.

Before this I believed that all churches were more or less the same, and I had no idea about what the gospel really meant, or the importance of religion. When I was about eleven I saw religion as something you did on Sundays. I knew who God was, I knew about Jesus and His disciples, Joseph and Mary, etc., but I didn't see their relevance in my life.

There was always a good atmosphere in the house when the Elders came to visit. One of the first things the Elders asked me to do was to try and pray. At first I found it hard to pray. Every time I knelt down, my conscience got heavier and heavier. To this day I still get pangs of remorse about my ill spent youth. When I look at younger people who were brought up in the Mormon Church, I feel happy for them. I see the way they lead their lives, and I think of what I was doing at their age . . . drugs, drink and women. It makes me feel dirty.

I was greatly impressed by the lifestyle of the people in the Mormon Church. The high standards they had. Their mutual respect. The genuine friendliness, the lack of bad language. There was an honesty about them which surprised me. They didn't need drink or drugs to have a good time.

Every eligible male from twelve years upwards has the opportunity to hold the priesthood. Initially in the Aaronic priesthood, and at the age of eighteen, in the Melchisedech priesthood. In other words it was a lay clergy, which meant that everybody had a normal job besides their Church calling. It amazed me that there was no paid clergy. This put the idea of "serving" and "service" into its proper perspective. It's one thing serving your fellow men when you're getting paid for it, but to serve without any payment is an entirely different matter. This was real service.

All these things contributed to my conversion. However, when I learnt about the purpose of life and my own self worth, I realised that I wanted to be a member of the Church. I wanted to live my life like that. I wanted to live by those standards. I'd wasted so many years of my life, and yet my life was just beginning.

My dad and Marina were delighted with my decision to be baptised. Looking at their happiness helped me to understand how the gospel can change your life.

When I told my mother about my decision she was a little bit startled. "I suppose you could do a lot worse." I laughed with her. Yes, I could do worse, and I did a lot worse. But living by gospel principles makes bad people good, and good people better.

On the 9th of February I was nervous. I'd bought a new suit, shoes, shirt and tie for the occasion. We arrived at the Church in plenty of time. Elder Conk and Elder Wilson were getting the baptismal font ready, and people started arriving. I was surprised by the number of people who turned up. Baptism in the Church is by total immersion (you get soaked!). As I was about to enter the baptismal font, my nerves disappeared. My friend Joe Shannon baptised me. I first met Joe shortly after the incident, and his advice to me at that time made a lot of sense. He was a sound chap. He worked in the Civil Service, but he was also responsible for the welfare of the young men in the Terenure branch of the Church. As I saw the happy faces of Elder Conk and Elder Wilson, I felt like a new man.

I found new friends in Church and in my running club. It wasn't easy at first. I was the new kid on the block. When I was using drugs I was able to talk to anyone or anything at raves, parties and clubs. Your inhibitions vanish when you're on Ecstasy. You become "Mr Friendly," "Mr Sociable." I could sit down beside the girl I hated the most and, at the end of the night, I could end up in bed with her.

Elder Conk and Elder Wilson helped me by introducing me to people of my own age. This was great, but I had to fend for myself in the running club. My appearance didn't help at first. I still had a gaunt look about my face, my hair was shabby, to say the least. I'd put a black dye in my hair to get rid of the platinum blonde. But I had dark roots and orange tips. But I did make friends with the lads and the girls in the running club. I remember one incident in the training hall. It was quite slippy around the edges. I did a little sprint but, as I slowed down, I fell flat on my ass. "Are you all right?" asked one of the girls.

"Yeah, I'm fine, thanks," I replied. My face flushed red. Talk about feeling embarrassed!

As time went on things got more relaxed. I made new friends, real friends. People I could relate and talk to about normal things and life in general, unlike the conversations of old.

"How much is it for those Es?"

"I was absolutely out of my head."

"Those Doves are well worth a score."

"Man . . . these things are only gorgeous."

I went to the dances in the Church. These were held every month. The first few felt weird to me.

They weren't what I was used to. The music, atmosphere and surroundings were so different . . . I felt like a fish out of water at first. But as I adjusted I began to enjoy them and have some really good fun.

Besides Church, the running club became my main social engagement. All my efforts were put into running. When I look back I realise I was fighting with myself. I was trying to prove myself to myself. It probably sounds a bit strange, but I guess you'd have to experience it to understand it.

I was still nervous about going out anywhere beyond Dundrum or Terenure. It didn't help when the running club moved their training out to the track in Belfield, Stillorgan. It was getting close to the summer, and the track was usually packed with athletes. I was on the track doing a few warm-up laps with some of the guys. Suddenly I saw Michael Flynn, Harry's older brother. I stopped running. Michael had been good friends with Bobby's older brother, and with Robin Murphy and Stockton! I kept looking around to see where he was . . . talk about paranoid, my nerves were shattered. I made an arrangement with the coach to do my training earlier on Wednesdays to avoid bumping into Michael. Luckily the coach agreed.

As the temperature started to rise, I knew that

summer was here. I began to get to know myself again . . . the me that existed before drugs. I realised what I wanted out of life. A good job, a wife and a family. I was really thankful for how far I'd come.

In June of 1995 I started writing this book. The idea first came from my counsellor, who suggested that it would be a good form of therapy. If I could put my thoughts and memories on paper, it would help me get them out of my system. Mary suggested that, if I wrote it, I should get it published because it would be a great help to concerned parents and people in her profession. At first I found it very difficult to gather my thoughts. There were days when I would sit down for about four hours, and only write one page. The beautiful warm summer weather didn't help matters. Racing picked up during the summer, and I was running at least once a week. At one of the races I met Harry's father. He told me that Harry had gone into St John of God's with a nervous breakdown. This was a huge shock to me. He explained that Harry had some sort of disease for a long time, but that it was dormant. Ecstasy and acid had sparked it off and accelerated its effect. It might not have manifested itself for another twenty years, but the Ecstasy and acid acted as a catalyst. I felt sorry for Harry, because we were best mates before the drug scene.

In July I was in the changing rooms at a race in Santry when suddenly Harry and his father walked in. "I don't believe it . . . aw, man," he said when he saw me.

"All right, Harry. How are things?" I asked.

"Not too bad. How are you . . . what are you doing out here?"

"I decided to take your brother's advice and get back into the running," I said.

"Good man . . . good man," he said.

I couldn't believe the difference in Harry. His face was very heavy looking. He'd put on at least a couple of stone in weight. He was obviously on medication, his speech was very slow and slightly slurred. This wasn't the Harry I had known. Harry was five foot nine in height, jet black hair, sallow skin with an Arabian look about him. He was the type of person who would walk into a club and half the women in the club would swoon at him. But he was indifferent to this, he wasn't an ego tripper. He'd often say to me, "Look, Madzer. All those girls are looking at you . . . you're a stud."

I'd reply with a box and tell him to cop on. For a couple of days after seeing him I had very vivid dreams of my old times with Harry.

When I had to stop running at the end of July, I began to find it easier to write this book although I found it difficult to concentrate for any length of time. It was only at night when I was in bed that the book came to life. All the memories would come flooding back, but in the morning I didn't find it easy to put them into words.

In September I was able to resume my running. It was so good to be back on the track again. The good weather in September and October made it easy to get back in shape. Our normal weather can be quite discouraging. Before I knew it I was hearing Christmas ads on the radio and on the television. Jamie was getting all excited about Santa Claus and the big day.

This Christmas felt very different from the last few years. I was here on earth with my feet firmly planted on the ground, and my head was attached to my shoulders. I wasn't thinking of how I was going to sneak out for a quick joint, or how many Es I was going to pop during the holiday period. My thoughts were on other more important things . . . family and friends.

FLASHBACKS

I've watched so many war movies in which people suffer the effects of post traumatic stress. They return to normal civilian life but they're constantly haunted by vivid images of war. I've never been in a war zone, in the normal sense of the word, but I've been in my own war zone . . . the drug culture. People who have never had the experience of flashbacks have no idea how serious and how *real* they are.

Once I was at the bottom of our road waiting for a bus. I lit up a joint. After a couple of puffs I felt really weird. My head was light. I started burning up all over. I broke out in a cold sweat. My vision blurred and the colours of the cars and the trees were fluorescent. A bus went past. It looked like a green light. I began wobbling and staggering. I crouched down on my knees and leant against the bus shelter. I felt sick. I thought I was going to puke. When I came around I was really shaken up. However, true to form, after another five minutes I finished off the joint!

It was well known among the drug users that taking acid greatly increased your chance of getting a flashback. LSD, or acid, is the main cause of flashbacks. If you take acid even once you have a great chance of getting a flashback sometime. Surely not after just once, you ask? People are under the illusion that if you take acid, just once, within a few days your body will have passed it out of your system. Wrong.

There is a test known as the Spinal Tap Test, which all pilots must take before receiving their flying licence. It involves tapping the bottom of the spine and, if you have ever taken acid into your system, it will show up on this test. Most of the acid is used up in the "trip", but there will always be a small residue that lodges in the base of the spine. I guess that rules out the airforce as a career for me.

Unfortunately these flashbacks don't just happen when you're awake. They can also strike when you're asleep. I've had many flashbacks since I started writing this book. Some of them would make a good horror movie. I remember one evening watching television with my family. The lead story on the news was about a major drugs seizure. Customs and police had seized 150 million pounds worth of cannabis in one swoop. My reaction to anything relating to drugs on television was to make a joke about it, or else to stay quiet with a lump in my throat. However, that night when I went to bed I had a most horrific nightmare. I was right back in the middle of it all again . . .

"Madzer, have you got the money for that bag of E?" screamed Stockton.

"Yeah, I just need a little more time . . . I just have to see somebody . . . " I pleaded.

"You've had enough time, Madzer. I need the money now!" Stockton roared.

"I haven't got it yet. Bobby has half the bag of E," I said.

"No he hasn't, you have it all. I want my money . . . now!" he bellowed.

"OK. I'll get it for you. I have it in the bank . . . let me go," I screamed.

"I'll squeeze the money out of your neck, Madzer," he growled as he lifted me off my feet by the throat.

"No, honestly . . . I'll get it for you. My dad will give me the money . . . let me go," I screamed.

"You've had long enough, Madzer. I'm going to smash your head in first." He cackled as he drew back his fist to punch me right in the face.

"No!"

My dad was touching me on the shoulder. "Julian, what's wrong?"

"What? Dad . . . oh, I was having a nasty dream. Phew, only a dream."

I told Dad about the nightmare, and he told me to forget about it.

"That's all in the past now, Julian. Just forget about it," he said.

With dreams like that, who cares if it's in the past, it felt like the present. I was in a cold sweat.

I don't know what sparks off these flashbacks. It must be something to do with the association of ideas. Sometimes it's after hearing rave music. Then again it can happen when I hear a conversation about drugs. One day I was travelling home on the bus. A guy lit up a joint in the seat right behind me. As the smoke wafted under my nose, I recognised the old familiar smell of hash. I broke out in a sweat. I was suddenly back in Murphys' house. I shuddered and got off the bus.

It's over a year now since I've touched any drugs, but the reminders are still all around me. I can't enjoy a bowl of strawberries and cream without thinking of Strawberries, the acid tabs. Every time I see a yin yang sign for martial arts or tai-chi, I'm reminded of the Yin Yang acid tabs. When I see the Microsoft logos on my computer, I think of the Microdot acid tabs. When I see capsules I think of "Dennis the Menace" Es. The simple Disprin tablet constantly reminds of the white dove E tablet. News items on television, headlines in the newspapers about people dying from Ecstasy – and I have flashbacks.

The last year has been tough for me and for my family. Because of my irresponsibility my life had to be run by my father. But now it's time for me to fend for myself. There was a time over Christmas when I went out to a social with the running club. After the social a few of us decided to go to my old rugby club to see an old friend of mine. It was good to see some of my old friends who weren't involved in drugs, but I didn't enjoy being surrounded by drunk people in a smoky atmosphere. I arrived home at three in the morning. The next morning Marina told me that my dad had spent most of the night worrying about me. I can understand his concern, and I appreciate his point of view. He's obviously afraid of me travelling that same road again. The fear and the hate that I have for the drug scene, the remorse that I feel, the flashbacks that I get, and the anger at losing out on so much of life during that period, is enough of a deterrent to keep me away from drugs for the rest of my life. It's taken me a year to get clean away from it. A lot of pain, time and effort has gone into that year. Would I throw it all away? Do I want to destroy everything that I've achieved this year? Do I want to let down all those people who have helped me get through this year? My answer is no, no, no. I am a new person. I don't want drugs to be a part of my life.

You can listen to all the reports, see the statistics, and listen to the doctors telling you of the dangers. But there is one important message I have for those people who are involved in the drug scene and want to get out of it – do it now! Don't wait until tomorrow or after the weekend . . . that weekend could make you a statistic. Believe me, it's just not worth it.

CHAPTER TWELVE

by Gerry Madigan

December '94 was the beginning of the end of a nightmare. Even though Julian was taking the first fragile steps on the road to recovery, there was an unbelievable sense of security in the knowledge that at least he was in the house. I was able to sleep soundly once again, knowing that all my children were in their own beds under my roof. Perhaps it may seem quite normal to sleep soundly at night, but when you've spent the previous few years anxiously awaiting the return of your son from a rave or a party, wondering, speculating, letting your imagine take over . . .

On Christmas Eve I overreacted when he arrived home fifteen minutes late. But I was terrified that it was going to start all over again. Since the incident with Stockton I was determined to save Julian from the drug culture, no matter what it took. Luckily he was willing to go along with everything and, as a result, he made tremendous progress.

However, the first month of 1995 was like watching a picture in slow motion. I had read about the after-effects of Ecstasy. I was worried that it had left Julian in a morose state of lethargy. It was pitiful to watch him move around the house in a daze. Marina and I were on constant phone duty to screen all calls that came for Julian. It was only when I put the word out that he'd gone to Australia that the calls stopped coming. We'd been receiving about ten calls a day since the incident.

Julian's behaviour was extremely worrying. He seemed to have lost interest in everything. He slept until about midday, and then spent about an hour pottering around the cooker making himself breakfast. He plonked himself in front of the television and watched videos for most of the day. He fell asleep about mid-afternoon whilst watching television. He was reluctant to go to bed. He developed a pattern of going to bed late and getting up late in the morning. We were all delighted that he had extricated himself from the drug culture, but we still hadn't got our Julian back . . . he was living in a world of his own.

It was difficult to restrain myself at this time. Part of me was so grateful for the small amount of progress that had been made, but another part of me wanted to shake him. He was obviously going through a type of cold turkey, and I guess he didn't know how to handle it. I gently encouraged him to go to bed earlier, and I began to call him earlier in the mornings. A beginning. We still had to get him involved in doing something with his time . . . anything!

I realised that this was going to be a long and difficult road. I became increasingly aware of the need for outside help. He had to learn to communicate again. He had to start mixing with people again. He had to start living again. His counsellor, Mary Cantwell Lynch, was having regular sessions with him. I could see that these sessions, although sometimes very difficult and emotionally draining for him, were helping him come to terms with his feelings. Liam Nicholson encouraged him to join the running club, and it was the best move Julian ever made. At last he had something to focus on.

He started having discussions with Elder Conk and

Elder Wilson, and they were a great help in getting him involved with guys his own age. He played basketball or football with them almost every week. Now he was beginning to come alive again. As he investigated his own beliefs he had to take stock of himself and ask himself some serious questions. He was using his brain again.

After the previous year of constant nagging and aggression, I had to become as gentle and placid as possible if I was to expect any real success from his efforts. I tried to be there for him, but more as an observer than a participant. I watched him slowly develop a relationship with the Elders, become more involved with his running club, and attend his regular counselling sessions. I began to see a change in his attitude. He began to communicate with the rest of the family. Tim, Jessica, Colin and Jamie had their big brother back again. He actually talked with Marina and me . . . this was progress!

When he became a member of the Mormon Church he began to make new friends. By March of '95 Julian was actively involved in regular social activities with his new friends, and he was going to his running club about four times a week. He had embarked upon a weights training programme, and he was watching his diet.

But there were occasional mornings that reminded me of the horrors of Ecstasy. I remember the look on his face and the pain in his eyes after one of his nightmares. They happen less frequently now, but they serve as a constant reminder of what it was like. Julian wakes up in a cold sweat after these ordeals, and it takes him most of the day to recover.

There is the ever-present danger of him meeting some of the old gang. He was absolutely shocked when he met Harry at one of his running meetings. Unfortunately Harry wasn't as lucky as Julian, they can never resume their friendship. Julian came home one day from a visit to his mother's. He looked pale and drawn.

"You'll never guess who I saw in town, Dad," he said.

"Who did you see, Julian?" I asked.

"I was travelling through town in the bus. I looked out the window and there was Stockton!"

"Did he see you?" I asked.

"No, he didn't. But my heart nearly stopped."

By May of '95 Julian was well on the way to recovery. I couldn't help feeling proud of him. This was my son whom I loved dearly, and whom I almost lost. He could have been one of the victims that I read about in the newspapers . . . "Boy dies from Ecstasy". I hated what he was doing, even though I had no idea how dangerously involved he was at the time. But I never stopped loving him. I could still remember the day in October 1975 when I carried him out of Holles Street Hospital wrapped in a little blue blanket. He was my little boy, and I didn't want to lose him. Now he was fighting to get himself back on track.

In 1994 and for the previous four or five years Julian smoked, drank, and abused drugs. These were all part of his normal routine. In February of '95 he had given up tea and coffee, stopped drinking alcohol, stopped smoking, and stopped using any sort of drugs. Initially I held my breath . . . but it lasted. He has put the past behind him. The rave scene is no longer a part of his life. His associates from the drug culture are no longer a part of his life. He has no desire to see them. His social life has changed radically. He now enjoys a night out in the company of his new friends without the need for alcohol or other stimulants. He has developed physically and he is running competitively once again.

Last May, when we were asked to attend a meeting of concerned parents in a local school, Julian was prompted to put his counsellor's advice into action and write this book. He couldn't get over their ignorance about the drug scene. He wanted to put his experiences in writing in order to help other young people who were caught in the web, and also to make parents understand what it's all about. But he found it extremely difficult to remember the last few years. The discipline and mental concentration of writing a book was a new departure for a brain that had been bombarded and abused by Ecstasy, acid, alcohol and hash for about four years! He started writing the book in June. It took nearly eight months for him to complete it. But he stuck with it and can now mark it up as another achievement in a year filled with changes for the better.

Christmas of 1995 was one of the happiest times of my life. I had my whole family around me. At times I'm almost afraid to blink in case I wake up and find that it was all a dream.

I recognised the need for a network of support in order to make Julian's recovery a success. It was the combined efforts of support and encouragement from his family, his counsellor, his coach, Liam Nicholson, Elder Conk and Elder Wilson, and his new friends in Church and at the running club. We had been missing Julian from our lives, and we had to show him that he had been missed. It was important that Mary Cantwell Lynch was there to listen to him, and to encourage him to get his life back on track. Liam

Nicholson showed Julian that he genuinely cared about him by his regular contact and enquiries about his progress. Eddie McDonagh, the coach in the running club, was an essential part of the recuperation. He made Julian feel welcome and part of the club, and gave him the alternative focus he badly needed. The Elders showed him genuine friendship and helped him to develop a spiritual dimension to his life. His new friends, in Church and in the running club have helped him to break out of the shell that he had built around himself in the drug culture. They helped him to interact socially again on a normal level without the use of stimulants.

Yes, it's been a great year, and now we can look forward to the future with hope and with confidence. I'm eternally gratefully to all those who helped bring Julian back from the brink. But I consider myself one of the lucky parents. I still cringe whenever I read a newspaper headline about another Ecstasy death. I empathise with those parents who have lost their sons and daughters. I get angry when I see people trying to glorify drug abuse, or play down the dangers of Ecstasy as "soft drugs".

My son is home safe, but there are thousands of young people still out there. Caught up and sucked into the social and emotional sub-culture that is destroying young lives, bringing heartache and suffering to parents, and devastating families. It is a pernicious evil that is pervading our society. It must be recognised for what it is.

The anxious ordeal of the last couple of years was horrific. But the story has a happy ending. One young man has been saved. Our family is intact once again. Thank you everyone who has helped in making this a success story. To all those young people still involved in Ecstasy and other drug abuse . . . please, stop taking the tablets.

FACTS AND FIGURES

Information and Statistics

Ecstasy: MDMA (methylenedioxymethamphetamine) Is an illegally manufactured chemical drug. A stimulant with amphetamine and mild hallucinogenic properties. It comes in tablet and capsule form. Unfortunately, you never know (until it's too late) whether or not you're getting pure MDMA. Ecstasy is one of the most adulterated drugs on the market. It has been known to contain LSD, caffeine, speed, anti-histamines, paracetamol, cold cure powders, morphine, barbiturates, ketamine and strychnine. Used extensively in rave and dance clubs, it allows the body to keep going at a frenetic rate long after it should have shut down.

Names of some popular Ecstasy tablets/capsules: Doves, White Doves, Mad Bastards, Dennis the Menace, New Yorkers, Disco Burgers, M&Ms, Shamrocks,

Rhubarb & Custards, Super Doves, Colliers, Lion Hearts, Speckled Doves, Love Doves.

MDA, the parent drug (methylenedioxyamphetamine), has different properties and effects.

MDEA, (methylenedioxyethylamphetamine) is another offshoot of MDA.

Amphetamine, (amphetamine sulphate): A manufactured stimulant drug that comes in the form of a white, grey, pink or yellow powder. Sometimes it comes in tablet or capsule form. It usually eaten or sniffed.

Some names of amphetamines: Billy, speed, sulph, whizz, amphet.

Acid: LSD (lysergic acid diethylamide), an illegally manufactured psychedelic/hallucinogenic drug that comes in the form of tiny transfers like miniature postage stamps. Normally these are eaten. Each tiny piece of this blotter-like substance contains about 75 micrograms of LSD. A regular postage stamp weighs about 60,000 micrograms.

Names of the various acid tabs: Strawberries, Gorbachevs, Microdots, Blotters, Acid, Drop, Lucy, Stars, Tab, Trip, Flying Keys, Test Tubes, Golden

Keys, Yin Yangs, Sperms, Swastikas, Purple Omes, Penguins.

Cannabis (Cannabis Sativa): The bushy Indian hemp plant grown in India, Asia and South America. It comes in three forms.

Cannabis Resin: This is scraped or squeezed from the plant and compressd into blocks that look like large bars of stock cube. It can be a yellow/green, brown or black colour, and goes under various names, e.g. blow, dope, draw, hash, hashish, Leb gold, Paki black, rocky, soap bar, squidgy, Moroccan. Normally smoked, but can also be used in food.

Cannabis Herb: Made from the leaves and flowers of the plant. When they've been dried and crushed they look like mixed herbs. Known as marijuana, grass, dope, ganga, pot, weed, skunk, Thai stick, super skunk. Normally smoked.

Cannabis Oil (Hash Oil): Liquid extracted from the plant and then concentrated into a black oil with the consistency of liquid tar. Rarely available. Names of cannabis smoking: joints, tokes, spliffs, reefers, joysticks.

THC (Tetrahydrocannabinol): The psychoactive chemical ingredient in cannabis. This remains in the fatty tissue of the brain and reproductive organs for several weeks.

Opium (Papaver somniferum): A plant grown mainly in Turkey and India. Narcotic drug produced from the drying resin of the unripe capsules of the opium poppy. Heroin, powder or dark brown solid, is smoked, eaten or injected. Methadone, a synthetic drug used as an alternative to heroin, is also addictive.

HELPLINE

Organisations/Associations/Treatment Centres for Drugs Awareness, Counselling, Therapy

Organisation	Address	Tel/Fax
EURAD *Europe Against* *Drugs*	Kilcullen House 1 Haigh Terrace Dun Laoghaire Co Dublin	Tel 284 1164 Fax 284 1577
Drug Treatment Centre	Trinity Court 30-31 Pearse St Dublin 2	Tel 677 1122
Health Promotion Unit *Information on Drugs*	Department of Health Hawkins House Dublin 2	Tel 671 4711
Anna Liffey Drug Project	13 Lower Abbey St Dublin 1	Tel 878 6899
Crosscare *Catholic Social* *Service Conference* *Drug Awareness Programme*	The Red House Clonliffe College Dublin 3	Tel 836 0011
The Talbot Centre	29 Buckingham St Dublin 1	Tel 836 3434
Narcotics Anonymous	13 Talbot Street Dublin 1	Tel 830 0944 Ext 486

Coolmine Therapeutic Community	Coolmine House 19 Lord Edward St Dublin 2	Tel 679 3765 Tel 679 4822
Garda Drug Squad	Harcourt Square Harcourt Street Dublin 2 Cork Limerick	Tel 475 1356 Tel 021 313 031 Tel 061 414 222
Mater Dei Counselling Centre	Mater Dei Institute Clonliffe Road Dublin 3	Tel 837 1892
Community Awareness of Drugs (CAD)	6 Exchequer Street Dublin 2	Tel 679 2681
The Rutland Centre Addiction Treatment	Knocklyon House Knocklyon Road Dublin 16	Tel 494 6358
BAD *Balbriggan Awareness of Drugs*	St Theresa's NS Balbriggan Co Dublin	Tel 841 1737
IACT *Irish Association for Counselling & Therapy*	8 Cumberland St Dun Laoghaire Co Dublin	Tel 230 0061
ALFA *Advisory & Counselling Services*	31 Weirview Drive Stillorgan Co Dublin	Tel 2880222
Parentline	Dublin	Tel 873 3500
Fr Joe Young	2 Donoughmore Cres Kincora Park Limerick	Tel 041 28 552

MAD *Meath Awareness of Drugs*	Marie Byrne The Aisling Centre Church Hill, Navan Co Meath	Tel 046 29 907
Laytown Against Drugs	Gerry O'Donoghue 4 Marian Villas Laytown Co Meath	Tel 041 28 552
Waterford Drugs Helpline	52 Upr Yellow Rd Waterford	Tel 051 73 333
Waterford Parentline	St. Brigid's Family Community Centre Yellow Rd Waterford	Tel 051 73 833
Galway Diocesan Youth Services	Yvonne Doyle Tagaiste House 4 St Augustine St Galway	Tel 091 568 483 Fax 091 563 321
Sligo Addiction Counselling	Brendan Courage Liz Sheridan 12 Johnston Court O'Connell St Sligo	Tel 071 43 316
Donegal Addiction Counselling	Hugh McBride St Conal's Hospital Letterkenny Co Donegal	Tel 074 21 022
Business Against Drugs	6 Kensington Court London W8 5Dl England	Tel 0171 937 8228 Fax 0171 937 9799

Lifeline	101-103 Oldham St	Tel 0161 834 7160
	Manchester M4 1LW	Fax 0161 834 5903
	England	
ISDD	Waterbridge House	Tel 0171 928 1211
Institute for the	32-36 Loman Street	
Study of Drug	London SE1 NEE	
Dependence	England	

A directory called "Drug Problems – Where To Get Help/ Guide To Services" is available from SCODA Publication Sales, 32-36 Loman Street, London SE1 NEE. It has approximately 500 listings in the UK, and it costs ST£5.50 plus ST£1.00 p&p.

Julian and Gerry Madigan present a comprehensive seminar on drugs awareness, based upon this book. They are both available for seminars, talks and workshops, and may be contacted at Paragon Communications, PO Box 3336, Rathfarnham, Dublin 16, Tel 494 7725 Fax 490 5975, or through the publishers of this book.

There have been over fifty **Ecstasy-**related deaths in Britain to date. Ten young people have died in Ireland, either directly or indirectly, from **Ecstasy**.

"What goes up, must come down."
. . . Theory of gravity
Sir Isaac Newton 1684

"If you don't like coming down,
don't get high in the first place."
Gerry Madigan 1996